Advance Praise for
The Coffee Shop Masquerade

"In The Coffee Shop Masquerade T.A. Morton skillfully weaves tales of love, loss, and self-discovery, reminding us of the profound impact even the smallest gestures can have on our lives. The Coffee Shop Masquerade is a poignant exploration of human nature, destiny, and the universal yearning for connection."
— Rosie Milne, Editor of the *Asian Books Blog*

"Deft, thoughtful, and eschewing cliché, T.A. Morton's slice of contemporary Hong Kong showcases her skills as a sharp social observer. While a cross –section of locals and expatriates struggles to survive financially, emotionally and physically, the coffee shop that connects them becomes a character in itself, reflecting the clashing moods and impulses of a city too busy for introspection. Morton is a talent to watch."
— Liz Jensen, Best Selling Author

The Coffee Shop Masquerade

T.A. Morton

The Coffee Shop Masquerade

By T.A. Morton

Trade Paper: 978-988-8904-25-9
Digital: 978-988-8904-24-2

© 2025 T.A. Morton

FICTION

EB227

Cover image made by CoverDesignAI, powered by Flux 1.1 Pro AI technology. Layout design finalised by Cordelia Wøidemann.

All rights reserved. No part of this book may be reproduced in material form, by any means, whether graphic, electronic, mechanical or other, including photocopying or information storage, in whole or in part. May not be used to prepare other publications without written permission from the publisher except in the case of brief quotations embodied in critical articles or reviews. For information contact info@earnshawbooks.com

Published in Hong Kong by Earnshaw Books Ltd.

For Thomas

"Culture is a mask that hides their faces. Here people showed themselves bare."
— W. Somerset Maugham

1

Providence

The further you travel, the less you know.
–Tao Te Ching

The first question was how did the mask end up here, sitting on a shelf behind the counter in a franchised coffee shop in Hong Kong?

Mario's Nonna, well, she would have said it was providence, god's order, his guidance. However, there were other unseen forces at work—it was destiny.

Mario was always receptive to her stories, and even if she did embellish from time to time, most of what she told Mario and his sister Veronica was true.

A man did leave the mask outside of a church one day in her hometown just south of Padua in Italy. She'd found it a week before she was married. Whether she spoke to the man who left it was irrelevant, in her mind anyway.

The mask came to live with her and her new husband. It was placed carefully on the wall in their large dining room—a sign of good luck, she had told him, like a horseshoe, but better. The mask hung on the wall and watched people come and go in daily life. It was a peaceful existence until Nonna had died a few months ago.

THE COFFEE SHOP MASQUERADE

Mario, now in his early 30s, was filled with grief. He decided to fulfill his promise to Nonna and took it back to what he had been told was its true home. Somewhere over there, Nonna had said, pointing, in the East, where their language was different, difficult, and filled with riddles.

Mario, now sitting in the Hong Kong coffee shop, was angry. He had just burned the tip of his tongue on the most awful cappuccino he'd ever had. He thought to himself, we have better coffee at the Auto Grills (service stations that dot Italian motorways). Why is it so hard to get decent coffee here? It's a major city, so surely there should be somewhere that doesn't sell this artificial junk.

He then groaned and felt the tip of his tongue with his finger, detecting a small bump. Ugh, just what I need.

He looked down at his watch—10 o'clock. It was another six hours until his first flight home departed, then another twenty until he would be physically home via Qatar and Rome to his small cramped one-bedroom flat in Padua.

He sighed—only a couple more hours left to hang around in this city that he had not enjoyed as much as he thought he would.

Yesterday, he told Veronica over the phone, 'It's dirty, like Rome.'

She tut-tutted. 'Don't be ridiculous. Hong Kong is nothing like Rome. What's wrong with you?'

He then stared out of his hotel window. 'I don't know. It's not like I thought it was going to be.'

'It can't be all sunshine and butterflies,' she replied playfully.

He smiled. 'You sound like Nonna.'

'Well, she had a point. You need more balance, Mario. You always have. You get too involved, and it takes over your whole life. You need to take a step back.'

'I'm taking a step back coming here, doing this crazy thing.'

He looked down at the mask sitting on the bed. He lifted it up, turned it around, and squinted, trying to decipher the small, scribbled writing on the back of it. *You can't read that*, Nonna's voice sounded in his head.

He placed it back on the bed. 'Veronica, do you think I'm stupid?'

'No, I don't.' She then paused. 'What you're doing is strange, but it has a purpose, right? A purpose for you to get out, get away. You've been much too sad — it isn't right.'

'I just wish, well, I wish you were here.' He then started to cry.

Veronica replied softly, 'I know, but Mario, you must do this for yourself. You always said that mask would take you places.'

He laughed. 'This stupid mask.'

'I blame Nonna. She filled us with too many stories about it. She said that she found this mysterious mask one day outside of a church, like it was waiting for her. Then a strange gentleman came up to her and told her that it was a magical mask, made in the East, very valuable and smuggled to Italy on a boat — a death mask of a young maiden killed by her jealous lover. An artist found it and painted over the original markings in white and gold so that it resembled a Venetian carnival mask, its true worth now hidden. The artist tried to sell it, but nobody wanted it, and he died penniless and starving. The strange man then found it years later and kept it until an angry spirit emerged from the mask — the dead maiden didn't like the garish colored paint. The spirit filled all his dreams with nightmares, she wanted to return home. The spirit told him that only a young girl could help her. One day, she'll need to go home to the East. And how did our Nonna help her? She hung it on the dining room wall to watch over us as we ate.' Veronica laughed.

Mario smirked, then replied softly, 'Do you remember when she told us about it?'

THE COFFEE SHOP MASQUERADE

'Right after papa died.'

'Strange sort of story to tell two children who had just lost their father.'

'Well, she was a strange sort of woman, wasn't she? Do you remember when she told us that the neighbor's cat was a reincarnation of Da Vinci, and she was convinced he was trying to communicate with us by always being on the roof?'

Mario laughed. 'The cat that wanted to fly like Da Vinci—he collected feathers. She said he was trying to make wings.'

'And the way she said he dug holes in her garden, like an artist. She said that he was Da Vinci himself! She was crazy, Mario!'

They both smiled, then there was a pause.

Veronica sighed. 'You can always come home, Mario.'

He stood up and stared out of the hotel window toward the Peak, which was covered in fog. 'This place is odd—it's filled with old and new, but it feels weird, like there are ghosts everywhere, and they're reaching out to us.'

'Well, like here then?'

'No, different, like the line between us and the dead is thinner here. Yesterday, when I went to the office to talk to that appraiser about the mask, it was like something out of a horror film. I thought it was an abandoned building, but there was a doorman who directed me toward the service elevator. I went up in this slow, old, rickety elevator, and the lightbulb kept flickering off and on. It was as if the whole place was about to be demolished. I came out of the elevator on the 10th floor, and it was empty, the paint peeling off the walls. I was about to go back into the elevator when I saw an old lady sitting beside the stairs. I smiled at her, and she nodded, pointing down the hallway. I said, 'For the appraiser?' She nodded. I walked past her to the end of the hallway and saw a gold-plated sign outside this thin wooden door. I knocked and entered, expecting it to be like the rest of the building—you know, in pretty bad shape—but it wasn't. Everything looked brand new. Glossy surfaces, mood lighting, wooden floors, glass doors to meeting rooms, and expensive minimalist furniture. So strange. This man comes out and bows; he's expecting me and leads me into a room that has no windows and is sealed. He locks the door, and the lights go off, then on again.

'You have the item?' he asked. I took out the mask and handed it to him. He placed it on a large table and examined it with a flashlight that beamed lights with different colors, I guess to verify the age or something. He moved it up and down and held the mask as if it was a newborn. He sighed a lot. I wanted to ask him about why he was in this sort of building, but I didn't want to disturb him. Twenty seconds later, he looked up, then handed me the mask.

'I'm sorry, but it isn't what you think.'

'Oh, it's not a Chinese death mask?'

He shook his head. 'No.'

I asked, 'Is it from here?'

'No, from the mainland. It's old, but not very valuable.' He stared at me and said, "You can pay on your way out." And, well, that was it.'

'Incredible story, Mario, but why didn't you ask him more about it?'

'I don't know. I didn't know what to ask, and he just seemed so sure it wasn't anything.'

'So, you flew 8,000 miles and paid 3,000 euros to find out that Nonna's mask was worth nothing? Mario, you have too much money and have too much imagination.'

'You know what was strange, though? When I was leaving, I spoke to the doorman downstairs. I asked whether this place was being renovated. He said no and that the tenant businesses liked it like that because people don't realize what's inside. He then looked around and whispered to me that the whole place is haunted. He hated doing the night shift and said weird things happen. He said they had an intercom system—you know, in case there was a fire—and sometimes he heard strange voices coming through it or laughter. At night, there are a lot of sightings—people who are seen, but not really here. The elevator sometimes randomly starts and goes to different floors, but nobody gets out or gets in.'

'So, it's haunted? Like most of Italy?' Veronica laughed.

'I suppose so.'

'What will you do with the mask now?'

'I don't know—take it home, I guess.'

'I'm sorry that it wasn't what you hoped, any of it, the city or the appraisal, Mario.'

'It's okay. I'm just glad I finally found out.'

Suddenly, there was a knock at his hotel door. 'I better go—I'll text you from the airport.'

'Ciao.'

Then there was another knock, and Mario rushed over. 'Yes, yes, I'm here.'

He opened the door to find a young man with a paper bag. 'Mario Risso?'

'Yes.'

'This is for you.' He handed over the bag.

'Thank you,' Mario replied.

The young man then walked away quickly before Mario could tip him.

Inside the bag was a heavy coffee-table book on Chinese masks. It contained large, full-page glossy prints of several masks, but no writing. He turned to the front page and read the badly scribbled inscription:

> *Masks look both in and out, Mr. Risso.*
> *Thank you for using our service.*

Both in and out? What does that mean? He went through each page carefully, examining each mask to find something similar to his, but there was nothing like it. Maybe they painted over the old drawings, he thought, or maybe there was no painting at all, and they didn't realize that.

He placed the book on the bed and looked at the mask.

He remembered asking, as a child, 'But Nonna, how can her spirit be trapped inside a mask?'

'Well, she's invisible, you see. She hides underneath the painting, but she likes it here in our home. She likes living with us, but one day, you must take her home.' Nonna said, sitting at the table while Mario tried to do his homework.

'Where's her home?'

'The East, as I told you before. China.'

'Can I see it, Nonna, the mask, up close?'

'Ah no. We must respect her. We don't want to upset her, do we? Or else we'll get no sleep. Now come on, Mario, how do we spell 'house'?'

Suddenly, the hotel room's phone rang, causing Mario to jump. He picked it up. 'Hello?'

'Checkout tomorrow, Mr. Risso, 10 a.m. We cannot offer you an extension, as we're fully booked. Thank you for understanding. Goodbye.'

He hung up the phone and sat down on the bed again. He should go out; it was his last night. But he didn't want to. He lay down.

Nonna's voice summoned him: *Come on, Mario. You didn't*

come all this way for nothing. Take her out and show her a good time.
He sat up and smiled. *Okay, Nonna, I will.*

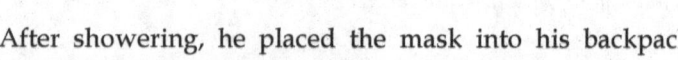

After showering, he placed the mask into his backpack and decided to go to Wan Chai, which he passed by yesterday in a taxi and regretted not stopping to check it out. It seemed alive.

He took the elevator down to Pacific Place and walked through the crowded mall toward Hennessy Road. It was busy as people scurried about, leaving work. He meandered through them and crossed the road. He started to walk through the streets and quickly located a small bar on Lockhart Road with a tiny outdoor seating area. It was empty, and he decided to sit down. An oversize fan was blowing on him.

Just one drink, he said to himself. I deserve at least one drink. It's been a while.

He considered taking the mask out and placing it on the table, but he didn't want to appear crazy.

'You aren't crazy,' Nonna had told him as a child after he came home crying because he couldn't read well. 'You just think differently, Mario. No one should understand everything. Where would the fun be in that?'

He ordered a draft beer from the young waitress with crooked teeth.

'Different,' 'weird,' 'crazy,' 'lazy,' 'stupid.' How strange to be labelled all these things when no one is the same; no one is normal. Everyone has something.

He opened his bag and looked at the mask. So, what if he's different, even eccentric? What's wrong with that? He was about to take it out when he heard a man yawn loudly. Mario turned and stared at him. He was a peculiar-looking man—dark and very hairy, wearing a gray suit that was too small for him. Mario looked him up and down and noticed that he was wearing two different-colored shoes, one brown loafer and one black brogue with no laces. He wasn't wearing any socks, and Mario glanced at his thick, hairy ankles.

The man noticed him. 'Hey, what you looking at?'

Mario turned away, embarrassed.

The man continued. 'Hey, you, with the mask.'

Mario turned to him, confused. 'Mask? What mask?'

'The one in your bag.' The strange man stood up and headed over to his table. He was average height, but his stomach poked out. He walked oddly — slumped over, his arms swinging. He sat on the empty chair opposite Mario.

Mario grabbed his backpack for protection and considered getting up, then the man said, 'I see your mask. Why you carrying around a mask like that?'

'What do you mean?'

'The mask. I know it. Doesn't belong to you.' The man frowned at him.

'Who does it belong to?' Mario asked.

'Not you.' The strange man grinned, and Mario noticed that his teeth were a sickly yellow and appeared deformed. He had large canines, almost like an animal, he thought.

The waitress arrived with the beer and placed it in front of Mario.

'Hey, girl, bring me another beer,' the man ordered.

She nodded, and as she walked away, the man slapped her on the bottom.

He giggled. 'Not much to look at in the face, but she would do.' He winked.

Mario stared at him, horrified. 'Don't you think you've had enough to drink?'

'Who me? No! I haven't even started.' The man sat back and

scratched his head, then rubbed underneath his armpits. 'So, where'd you get the mask?'

'My grandmother. She found it in Italy.'

The man then burst out laughing. 'Italy?'

'Yes,' Mario replied. He thought that this man belonged in some sort of freak show, like they had in the past—inappropriate exhibitions of people with exceptional biological differences. He was extraordinarily hairy, and his mannerisms, the way he scratched himself, almost like an animal.

'Well, well, that's where it's been.' The man stared at Mario.

'Do you know the owner? Who is it?'

'No one you know,' said the man, sticking out his tongue like a child.

Mario shook his head. 'You're crazy.'

He was about to get up when the strange man leaned forward and said softly, 'Hey, don't go, stay. We'll drink, and I'll tell you who owns it.'

Mario looked at him. As Nonna said, 'Everyone is different. It wouldn't be any fun if we were all the same.'

'Okay,' Mario replied.

The strange man grinned.

'So, who owns it?' Mario asked.

'Not yet, and from what I see, it isn't about who owns it. It seems to own you, carrying it around as if it's your girlfriend.' The man laughed loudly in short rhythmic bursts. Mario watched as he opened his jaw wide, and he could see all the way into his throat. *He really is like some sort of animal. Darwin's missing link? In Hong Kong?*

Mario cleared his throat. 'What do you know about the mask?'

The man looked away from him. 'Nothing much—only, well, you can't get much money for it now. No one has any interest in that sort of thing here. Too busy on their screens to realize the importance of other things. People always looking down, never up and forward. I saw one man get killed last week 'cause he was looking down. Silly boy.'

Mario watched as the man started to twirl the long hair on the side of his face. 'What's your name?' he asked him.

'People call me Monkey—well, they used to. Monkey, the great sage equaling heaven.'

Mario laughed, but Monkey looked down as if he was hurt.

'Do you like being called Monkey?'

Monkey looked at him curiously. 'I don't know. I never thought about it. Everyone has always called me Monkey—I never disputed it. What do they call you?'

'Mario.'

'Mario with the mask.' Monkey smiled.

Mario nodded.

Monkey finished his beer and looked at Mario's full glass. 'Shall we have another one?'

Mario called the waitress over.

They sat there together for three hours drinking beer quickly. Mario started to slur his words. He told Monkey everything about his Nonna, the mask, his obsessions with things. 'Once I start with something, I can't stop. It's not good. My sister says I need balance. I thought coming here and trying to find out about the mask would help, but it hasn't. It has made things more confusing.'

'Life is like that,' Monkey replied. 'The more you try and understand things, the less you know. You know, you should leave the mask with me. I can give it back to the owner.'

'Who's the owner? I want to meet him.'

'How you know it is a man, maybe it is a woman? And well, she isn't here now, but I can give it to her, weaver girl. Let you get rid of that thing. Help you get your balance back by no longer carrying it with you.'

Mario drunkenly agreed. 'That's exactly what I need. Balance—no more silliness.'

So, it was agreed.

Monkey said he would walk Mario back to the hotel. Intoxicated, they stumbled through Hennessy Road and up Justice Road. They sniggered like children at the smallest things, and Mario thought he never wanted this night to end. He realized he hadn't laughed like this in years.

Once they reached the hotel's grand lobby, Monkey stopped and looked fearfully at the hotel's entrance.

'Come on, Monkey, let's get a drink,' Mario said, waving him in.

'I can't. They don't allow me in here.'

'Come on, you're with me. It'll be fine.'

Monkey replied earnestly, 'No, I'll get in trouble again.'

Mario frowned. He was about to drag him by the arm, but stopped when he saw that Monkey was shaking. 'Don't worry, Monkey. It's okay,' he said.

He removed his backpack, but his footing faltered, and he nearly fell over.

Monkey remained in the shadows, away from the lights.

A doorman saw Mario fall out of the corner of his eye and ran toward him. 'Sir, sir, are you okay?'

'Yes,' Mario replied, annoyed, and stood up, 'I just needed to give this to my friend.' He glanced up, and Monkey has gone. 'Huh? Where is he?'

'Who, sir?'

'My friend. He was just here.'

'There's no one.'

'Yes, I can see that, but there was someone. Ugh, you scared him away.'

'Shall I take you inside Sir?'

'Monkey?!' Mario shouted 'Monkey?! You there? You want the mask?'

Mario staggered around, shouting. He halted when he saw an audience of well-dressed people staring at him.

'My friend, he's gone,' he said to them.

Some of them smirked back, but most looked down, fearful of acknowledging him.

'Maybe he will come back tomorrow, sir,' The doorman said, hopeful.

'Maybe.'

Mario entered the hotel quietly, went to his room, lied on the bed fully clothed, and fell asleep quickly.

In the morning, when he awakened, he felt oddly fine. He sat up and checked his bag. The mask was still there. He took a shower and considered that perhaps he had imagined it all, but he couldn't have. Wan Chai, Monkey, the waitress with the crooked teeth. After breakfast and checkout, he left his bag at the hotel and walked the same route through Pacific Place, crossed Hennessy Road, then on to Lockhart Road. He located the small bar where they had sat. It was closed, and all the furniture was piled up. Mario stood close to where they sat the previous night. He looked around, but there was no sign of anyone. He stared at the floor and noticed that it recently had been washed. He called out, 'Hello? Anyone there?'

But there was no reply.

He decided to take a taxi to Soho, after he read about it online. Listed as number 12 in the top 12 things to do in Hong Kong, it was an area filled with independent coffee shops, pop ups, bars and the famous outdoor escalator. Mario had wanted to see it and jumped in a taxi all the while keeping an eye out for Monkey.

The taxi dropped him off by Hollywood Road and Mario

walked up towards the escalator. It was warm and he needed something to drink. He saw a small coffee shop on the corner next to the escalator and entered. He looked around, it was quiet. He could only see one member of staff, she was reading a book by the cash register. He went over and ordered an espresso and waited patiently as it was made. He sat close to the main door and looked outside at the passing traffic.

'Monkey,' what an odd sort of nickname, grossly inappropriate. But how odd he was — the clothes, the shoes, the long hair — not fur, but similar. Mario sipped his espresso and tutted, it was horrible, and he decided to try another coffee shop. . But before he left, he asked the girl behind the counter whether she knew anyone called Monkey — maybe he was known in the area.

'Excuse me?'

She looked up at him; her name tag read 'Ruth.'

'I know this is going to sound strange, but have you heard of a man called Monkey who lives around here.'

She stared back at him, 'Monkey?'

'Yes, a strange-looking man, different-colored shoes, gray suit too tight for him. He has a lot of hair — well, a bit like fur.'

'Fur?'

'Yes. Do you know anyone like that?'

She shook her head and put down her book.

He looked at the title, *Wu Ch'êng-ên, Monkey*. Mario stared at her, surprised.

She followed his eyes to the book. 'Oh, it's an old myth about the Monkey King. He is a legend from the past.'

'I see.' Nonna's voice sounded in his head: *There are no coincidences, only providence.*

'Hey, listen, do you have a lost-and-found box? I just found this mask in the corner over there.' He pointed at the red couch and pulled the mask out of his bag.

'You found this over there?' Ruth replied suspiciously.

He nodded and handed over the mask.

Ruth handled it carefully. 'Is it valuable?'

'I'm not sure, but maybe. Maybe the rightful owner will come back for it.'

She looked at Mario. He seemed normal, but this was odd, something about him was strange. 'Hmm, are you sure you found this over there?'

'Yes, I am. Why would I lie?'

Mario then smiled at her and walked toward the door. A young man named Chris was walking in, and Mario held the door open for him.

'Ciao!' Mario said loudly.

Chris stared at him, confused. 'Ciao,' he replied back.

Ruth ran her fingers over the back of the mask and squinted at the small writing,

玉皇
Yù huáng

She thought, Jade Emperor? She shook her head and carried it to the lost-and-found box. She hid it under an umbrella and a set of keys that were left last month.

People are crazy. Why would someone leave a mask like this?

2

SINCERE

Sincere words are not pretty.
Pretty words are not sincere.
    –Tao Te Ching

Chris liked to do things a bit differently. He'd never downloaded a dating app and had been proud of it. He had preferred to meet women in person, by chance. He had believed in providence and, well, despite it having worked in his favor before, it hadn't worked since he'd arrived in Hong Kong. But he had hoped that it would all change now.

Before he entered the coffee shop, Chris was at home sitting on his secondhand couch reading the personals in the classified ad section in the newly launched *HK* magazine. There was one ad that he had been obsessing about over the past two weeks, and he read it again:

> Sincere, honest, Philippine girl seeks white European man 21–50 n/s for friendship + more.

He stared until the words appeared hazy, making his eyes feel heavy, like his head when he had listened to Wagner too early in the morning, the hammers and shouts pounding selfishly and disrupting his own easy flow. It was after watching the documentary about Wagner that the need to educate himself about classical music pressed itself upon him. Wagner—the first in a long, endless line of great composers—seemed the safest to start with. After all, he had viewed the madness, the ego, the genius in the hour-length program. Wagner's dramatic marches evoked childhood memories of visiting his uncle, who was once in the military service, and family days spent climbing on retired tanks and guns on exhibition outside the captain's office.

Chris had thought about entering the service in an attempt to start a family lineage of military tradition, but his weak eyes had let him down, along with his fear of being shouted at, a trait left over from the beginning of secondary school. Streams of tears would flow down his face as his science teacher screamed at his stupidity, at his weakness for not being able to identify the different parts of a cell correctly. Sometimes he would run out of the room, while other times, he just sat and lowered his head as his teacher brutally mocked his homework. Chris learned quickly to adapt, control his tears, and wait until the teacher moved on. He remained as passive as he could at school, allowing him to do pretty well in all other subjects.

Biting down on his nails anxiously, he closed his eyes and sat back on the couch.

The words sounded out in his head:

Sincere, honest, Philippine girl seeks white European man 21–50 n/s for friendship + more.

He had come to believe that this simple ad might provide him with the push he needed, a nudge toward sexual success and possibly something more. Through their simple flirtation, he falsely expected greatness, a chance at true love. He had Googled some of these words:

sincere
/sɪnˈsɪə/

adjective
1. free from pretense or deceit; proceeding from genuine feelings.

honest
/ˈɒnɪst/

adjective
1. free of deceit; truthful and sincere.
'I haven't been totally honest with you.'

Genuine and truthful, that is what he wanted and finally, the day had come when he was going to meet the ad's author.

He sighed and decided he would be better off going out, away from the words, the erotic hopeful feeling — out to where he easily could fall prey to distraction. Grabbing the torn classified page, he folded it gently and placed it in the deep pocket that lined his cargo shorts.

Leaving his small apartment that sat in the middle of a high-rise in Happy Valley, he hardly made a sound. The building's other occupants were still deep in the lull of sleep. It was Sunday morning, and the day's air hit him with a thud, already thick with heat. It was an odd occurrence of a warm January morning, its heat unwelcoming in the seasonal shift.

He checked himself in the mirrored windows of shops he passed by. His reflection, indented tinted glass distorting his view, allowed him to remain oblivious to the purple jam stain in the middle of his white polo shirt. Tiny sprinklings of hair follicles covered his head like dark dust, making his head appear larger than it was. His body, swamped in oversized clothes, appeared out of proportion with his skinny arms, swollen belly, and small legs. He failed to see the frail old woman inside one of the shops watching him while she took a break from running a vacuum cleaner over the shop's carpet.

He reached the tram stop, and strangely, there was one standing there as if it was waiting just for him. He leapt on it with nervous energy and sat on a skinny wooden bench. He exhaled loudly as the tram started to roar its way toward Queens Road Central. The warm breeze helped calm his nerves as he started to count the number of stops, a trick he often used sometimes to occupy his anxious mind. However, after the counting, the slim bench became uncomfortable underneath him, so he stood up and rocked with the tram's chaotic rhythm.

Suddenly, he arrived at his stop. He was far too early, and he jumped out hesitantly. Central was empty except for a pair of red taxis and a lone woman with an enormous straw hat collecting cans. The newly washed streets and closed shops appeared hostile, hidden behind their shaded doors and clean screens. Heavy scaffolding protruded over the road, making it feel cramped and disorienting, Chris felt as if he was standing in the middle of a large, warm box.

The moment of distraction on the tram had freed his mind, but the pressing matter that he was finally going to meet her—quite possibly the love of his life was now returning fast. He wanted to ignore it, but it came like a surge of thick arousal, like an annoying twitch that cannot be controlled. He thought fast about what to do. His mind quickly brought forth a distant memory—a stone staircase somewhere in the back, near Kennedy town, and he started to head toward it.

THE COFFEE SHOP MASQUERADE

He had taken this route once before, but that was when he had just arrived, and he was slimmer. Back then, he ran up the stairs with ease, but today, as he looked up at the awkward gray stairs, he grew anxious. He started running up fast and quickly became breathless. The uneven, jagged, concrete stairs and his excess weight made him feel nauseous. His body compelled him to halt. Grabbing a thin tree, he attempted to cough away the surge of vomit brewing in his throat. A stream of water began to flow down his back, and he silently cursed himself for not taking a taxi. Exhaling through this moment, he successfully eliminated the hack. Chris didn't notice that he was being watched by a local old man staring out of his small bedroom window that overlooked the concrete mass. He didn't see the old man smile towards him as he bent over the tree.

A tiny sign reading 'Caine Road' emerged from a steel pole on the next stair pointing its arrow up. It was like a holy vision to him, and he mustered up the little remaining energy he had to continue the ascent. Running up the last 10 steps, he reached the summit just in time to encounter two pretty Western girls running. He smiled at them, proud in using this last surge of energy. Very rarely did it happen so effectively, he thought, as he stretched out his legs. Looking down at the stairs, he shook out the final bouts of dizziness, turned, and walked toward the outdoor escalator.

A tiny 7-Eleven stuck in the middle of two dry cleaners was opened, and he hurried in. Ignoring the shop's Indonesian assistant, he took a small bottle of distilled water from the fridge and drank its contents in a matter of seconds. He winked over at the boy's amazed eyes and threw down some coins. Satisfied, he made his way down the road.

He passed an array of different shops—more dry cleaners, takeout restaurants, and unopened supermarkets with their pristine white shutters. He thought, if this were at home, these shutters would've been covered in all sorts of obscene graffiti. Images of ugly-looking teenagers invaded his mind; he could see them standing on a street corner with a can of paint arguing whether it was better to spray or sniff it. It occurred to him that he didn't see images like that here. Of course, it must go on somewhere, perhaps over in the wilds of Kowloon, but no vivid, familiar images came to him. In fact, the only time he had noticed teenagers was when he mistakenly went to Causeway Bay on a Saturday to pick out cheap IKEA sheets. The place was flooded with them — with their strange, cool glasses and giant T-shirts — they filled the streets, the skinny boys standing purposely gawky, desperate in their attempts to make the skinny girls laugh.

During his first few days here, he remembered feeling surprised that things were so chaotic and dirty, but after a few short months, he realized that everything had its system, and now he would often get a whiff of bleach or disinfectant filtering out of the air vents whenever he was in small shops or on the spotless MTR.

Relaxed in the safety of random thoughts, he strolled along and marveled at the grand marble entrances to the enormous luxury apartment buildings, their colors efficiently reflecting the increasing heat. The pale green iron stairs led to the outdoor escalator; its overpass lined with flower baskets filled with wilting petunias. A flock of small rock sparrows pecked away at the remains of a dropped sticky bun that someone had placed on the flat handrail.

Chris' thick gold chain bounced gently beneath his white polo shirt as he started to jog down the stairs confidently, gravity helping to carry his weight. Finally, he reached the coffee shop on the corner, he attempted to open the glass door, but it was locked. He squinted and looked in, he heard a noise from a distant vacuum cleaner somewhere inside.

Sighing, he looked around at the empty streets. He knew this area well, frequenting the busy streets of Soho almost every weekend. More than likely, he would be at Staunton's Wine bar or sometimes at the cheap Italian restaurant on the left side of the street, and occasionally he'd brunch with the rest of the Westerners on a Sunday in the overly colorful Australian restaurant. He was always with people—mostly work colleagues, but sometimes with visitors from home. Comfortable in their presence, he would laugh along with the others, with his head stretched back and his mouth opened wide.

Most weekdays, he joined his colleagues in Wan Chai, where he drank and conversed with the Filipina girls at Fenwick's Bar—small painted girls with large smiles who filled the bar's dark basement on weekends. Obvious in their quest to lure men, with their poor Versace imitations made with cheap fabrics draped scantily over their tiny frames, they all wanted money and security.

Chris was amazed at how his brother (just over for a week's holiday) managed to convince some of these girls to go home with him. Chris could never do this, and that was the problem. Of course, he had been approached, even offered a night's company more than once. In the past there had been a little intimate kissing, a little harmless handholding, but nothing of real substance, nothing of what he craved. His failure at this annoyed him to no end. He tormented himself. Why was it so hard for him? Why couldn't he allow their interest to arouse in him what he needed? He found them attractive and had no ties with anyone at home in England. In six months, he would be forced to renew his contract out here. But still there had been no one.

He kept that fact closely to himself. His brother embarrassingly had put him on the spot about all of this in front of his work colleagues one night in Wan Chai. Chris, afraid of losing face, decided to play along, and invented some seedy story. They drunkenly absorbed his lies as their drowsy thick eyelids widened to show their admiration of his sordid adventures, unaware that he had relayed scenes from his favorite Pornhub video. He felt confident in their respect. They believed his sexual exploits, so why not let them believe? To add to this shame, his brother, on his final night, ended up bringing two girls home, begging him to share his prize. Chris declined, instead he decided to spend the remainder of the night in his room drowning in vodka, numbing another failure.

Hopefully, this was about to change. As of the last Saturday of December, he picked up the newly vamped *HK* magazine while absorbing another fatty brunch. His greasy fingers smudged the glossy cover, as he scanned the articles. The black-and-white classified section fell out onto the floor. He bent over and picked it up. Scanning the employment section, he reached the personal ads and started to judge the adverts, but then stopped at:

Sincere, honest, Philippine girl seeks white European man 21-50 n/s for friendship + more.

'Sincere.' The word seemed to speak to him, it opened up within him something different. He felt himself sit up and lean into it, something real, a word that appealed to his soul, his thinking. It was like hearing a new song for the first time and loving its beat, although you were still unfamiliar with its voice. Sincere. He understood that it appeared to be what was lacking in the girls whom he met. The girls of Wan Chai appeared too keen, too fake, too interested. Perhaps this girl was like him, trying to find some sincerity in a jungle of easy sex. He convinced himself that she would be different, more genuine, game for a laugh—a girl he could see a couple of times a week who would stay over and cook with him. He became overwhelmed with this fantasy's intensity, and he quickly asked for the bill.

Chris left the café with the classified section and decided to walk towards home through the botanical gardens and allow the thought to crack open in his head like a fresh nut being cracked too early, its fruit still growing. He simply plucked it out and devoured it. The bells rang out from the church attached to the school at the bottom of Robinson Road, and he stopped, alert to the group of Philippine women young and old exiting the colonial church. Some held hands innocently, passive, still entranced by the service. They seemed a million miles away from the brittle smiles of their nightly cousins. He considered that this sincere girl would be more like one of these good girls. He followed some of them, fresh from Mass as they bounced down the hill their arms carried towels, cane mats, and plastic bags filled with lunch and two-liter Coke bottles filled with thick cordials. They looked like they were heading to the beach, but they settled themselves in one of the large grand entrance squares of a major bank. Their voices squawked away, resonating against the enormous steel, concrete, and glass that adorned the colossal building.

He returned home that Sunday and left the page of the classifieds opened on his small cream chair, he re-read its message, which again spoke to him.

Should I just do it and call her? Isn't it normally sad old men who call these lines? He wasn't sad, he thought—he was quite a catch, a world traveler. I'm as normal as anyone, but that word, 'sincere,' that's all I want, he realized. His veins grew warm over the prospect of calling this number.

What would he say? It would be a message service, and he would need to be brief, polite, and say something about sincerity.

Should he do it? He spent the remainder of that Sunday trying to talk himself into it.

It wasn't until late that evening, after giving into the persistent calls from his colleague begging him to go down to Delaney's pub for a pint, that he finally grabbed the courage and called. He tapped in the number and it rang. There was some message that he couldn't hear because of a fight around the corner, then suddenly a beep, and he was on:

'Oh, hi, hi. I'm Chris. I'm English. I'm 33, and I'd really like to maybe meet up with you. I'm also looking for something that's sincere, and you don't have to worry cuz I'm not one of those weird guys. I'm well, well, I consider myself pretty normal and nice, of course. So, if you want to give me a call, great. If you don't, no worries, but it would be great to hear from you. Yeah umm ... I work in Wan Chai, so maybe we could meet up here or somewhere else? Okay, well that's it, I think. Hope to hear from you soon. Cheers, bye. Oh, wait here is my number... Cheers, bye.'

He had done it, and all things considered, he thought he had left a pretty good message. Short and to the point, and how much can you learn about a person over the phone anyway? He walked back into the pub elated and proud of himself, but wisely remained silent about this action.

The next day at work, he checked his phone constantly. Nothing. After a couple of hours of silence, feelings of regret started to germinate within him. He felt like a moron, but eventually told himself to shut up, what's done is done, and that it would be only a matter of time. She would call — she had to. Sincerity wasn't that easy to find.

Then, on that Friday evening, when he was halfway through his fourth pint in a bar on the top of Lan Kwai Fong, she called him.

'Hello, Chris?' spoke a very soft Filipina voice.

'Yes!' he replied loudly as he fought his way out of the pub.

'My name is Candy. I girl in magazine.'

'What? Oh, bloody hell, hold on a minute.' He left the bar and was faced with a mob of Western drinkers in the streets of Lan Kwai Fong.

It was one of those nights when the city was alive, all ready to celebrate, conversing and exchanging stories, making it feel like a belated New Year's Eve without the countdown. He walked past a man dressed like the Monkey King and smiled at him. Chris admired his costume; he really did look like the Monkey King from the old TV show, with a small, gold crown gracing his head. Tourists surrounded him and took pictures, some handed him money. Chris heard him say, 'I'm Monkey, the great sage equaling heaven.'

This caused the crowd to laugh.

'Hold on, hold on,' Chris said into the phone as he ran down past the restaurants that lined Rats Alley. He found a quiet corner leading to an area where people practiced Tai Chi, beside a large garbage depot that was never opened.

'Yes, sorry, love. Who are you?'

'Candy, my name Candy.'

Chris answered, 'Yes, love?'

'Yes, my name Candy. I call you to meet with you, if you like.'

'Okay, excellent. I was worried when you didn't call.' He then smiled, elated, his body was alive with nerves.

'Please talk slowly. I not understand so much fast.'

'I ... was ... worried ... when ... you ... didn't ... call,' he replied, stressing the words.

'Hmm? I not understand.'

Chris rolled his eyes — this was going to be fun. 'Where would you like to meet?'

'Yes, meet, Sunday, at coffee shop next escalator, Staunton

Street.'

'Okay, great, what time?'

'Ten in morning time?'

'Yes, that's good.'

'Okay,' she said, then there was silence. Chris looked around, thinking of what to say when she started again,

'Okay, what clothes you wear?'

'What, now?' He looked down at his own jeans that were stained from the Thai curry he just finished.

'No, Sunday.' Candy erupted into a fit of giggles.

'Oh, right, I see what you mean, umm, I guess white polo shirt and shorts.'

Two Western girls in high heels overheard him and sniggered as they walked past. Chris gave them the finger and watched with satisfaction when one of them tripped over the uneven cobblestones.

'Okay, Chris, I wear pink top and blue jeans, okay?'

'Yes, okay.'

'Okay, Chris, you are English?'

'Yes, I'm English.'

'Okay, see you tomorrow. Okay?'

'Okay.'

'Okay, bye-bye.'

'Bye, love.'

Well, she sounded okay. Her English wasn't the greatest, but it's hard over the phone. Right, Sunday is the day, he thought. Filled with enough beer to keep him excited about the promise of sincerity and the chance that he might be able to complete the task at hand at least once, he decided to play sensible and leave early that night.

THE COFFEE SHOP MASQUERADE

But now it was that Sunday, with less than an hour to go. The signs of Soho hung above him. In the quietness of the early morning, their bright, loud colors appeared murky and felt intrusive. Their stylish lettering overlapped each other and confused the road's sequence.

Chris wandered aimlessly, contemplating her. His hands became cloaked in sweat with the possibility of sexual activity. The feeling throbbed throughout his being, it saturated him in excitement as he circled the streets. Everything felt off balance as he tried to calm himself. He stopped suddenly, trying to collect himself, but every breath encouraged more wanting, more excitement, and he began to feel nauseous and dizzy. He hadn't even met her yet, and he was already in a frenzied state.

He slowed down, then sat on a bench in the shade, took out his phone, and started to flip through football reels, which led to reels about how to know when someone finds you attractive, then reels about how to last longer in bed. He quickly grew tired, as none of this helped to distract him.

He looked back toward the coffee shop and decided that enough time had passed, and it was safe to return, with less than an hour to go. With every step he took back toward the shop, the need pulsated within him, turning his anxiety into excitement. She's the one, she has to be, he thought. He pictured her petite, naked body sitting on top of his, her tanned arms massaging his chest. He smiled to himself.

Chris sauntered over to the coffee shop carefully, as if he was being watched. He was about to push the door open when it opened itself, as Mario exited. 'Ciao,' he said grinning.

'Ciao,' Chris replied, confused. He noticed the girl behind the counter and the mask she was examining. It was an ugly mask, he thought, why is it here? He scanned the coffee shop, but couldn't see his girl, Candy, and he stood uneasily. His eyes glanced shyly over the other customers, but none of them stood out, they looked like staged mannequins, their presence no more than a backdrop to their meeting.

The aroma of strong coffee made him alert, yet distant, his mind once more preoccupied with time.

Thirty minutes to go.

Twitching fingers hidden in his short pockets gave away his nervous state. He breathed out slowly, trying to appear relaxed. He faced a magazine stand and looked down at its contents. Seeing yesterday's newspaper with a picture of a tram on the cover, his thoughts returned to the morning, the journey here, and the state of the trams. It amazed him to think that they were still going after all these years, one of the few things that had lasted within this island's vortex of constant construction and renovation. They were part of a resilient minority.

He sighed and headed toward the red faux leather couch. He sat down and grabbed the newspaper from the small coffee table in front and read the somber headlines.

Two more suspected cases of the new virus were reported on the Bernard Shaw estate in Tsuen Wan. He started to read the article with genuine compassion, but it wasn't until he was halfway through the story that he realized that he hadn't really read a word.

Feelings of apprehension had begun to rise within him, as he looked down at his fake silver Rolex, its fat face lying across his brown arm.

Twenty minutes to go.

As he put down the newspaper, he considered purchasing something to legitimize his stay. Oblivious that his back left an invisible indented sweat mark on the red faux leather couch, he walked over to the empty counter, he loudly ordered something ice cold.

THE COFFEE SHOP MASQUERADE

'Iced latte, please.' He picked a grande size.

The girl behind the machine directed him to the tiny round table at the end of the counter. He grabbed a sugar sachet and started to beat it on the counter gently. Voices sounded around him; a noisy jazz composition and the bang of the espresso machine, made it seem as if all were in sync, performing a weird experimental melody. His iced latte landed on the stained wooden counter. Grasping its slippery sides tightly, he headed back toward the red couch, then stopped and changed his destination after he saw an elderly couple making their way to his spot. They were well-dressed, but slow. A table with two skinny cane chairs beside the entrance was free, and he sat down, facing the door.

This is better, a good spot, he thought, I'll see her first. A happy morning couple then passed him: The woman's arms were filled with sunflowers, and it occurred to him that he should've bought her a flower—a rose or something. But that's not my style, he thought. He wasn't like that. He remembered his dad saying to him, 'Be careful whom you buy flowers for, son, for they'll always expect it.' His dad was right. What if he didn't like this girl? He didn't want to appear overconfident, that he was trying too hard.

He sat silent, and took lengthy sips of his iced latte. Looking around, he scanned the mural that contained large scribbles of oversize coffee cups, the thick, black lines muted by a wash of warm greens and oranges. A gold arrow pointing left sat in one corner, with the word 'taxi' scrawled underneath. It looked like something they would have in an airport, he thought.

Restless, he started to analyze people in the coffee shop. The elderly couple on the red couch appeared busy sharing a huge Danish pastry. A Western girl with bad skin sat in a corner munching away on a muffin while reading some celebrity magazine. Two locals sat together, but both separately stared intently into the screens of their phones. They looked like brother and sister, but probably were married, Chris thought.

Slurping away at his cold, sweet latte, he let his feet tap away to the old jazz beat.

Suddenly, the door opened, and five people entered together. He cringed at their foul language and the roughness in their voices.

Then suddenly,

'Hello, Chris?'

He looked up and met her eyes. They were young and sweet. He smiled and knocked over his chair as he stood up to greet her. She giggled as he bent over to pick it up. He glimpsed up at her quickly; she was tiny. Her nylon, pink tube top stuck to her skin, outlining her thin frame. A pale line of discolored, charred pearls fell from her top, covering the little skin emerging from her navel. Her jeans were tight, their top covered in a confused glitter flora design. Her black plastic sandals were about three inches high. Her clothes looked worn, bordering on shabby. Her hair was down, long and elegant, but her face—above those young eyes lay thick pale-pink eye shadow, and her cheeks were densely rouged. She had attempted to cover her tiny spots with cheap foundation that was too pale for her, making her appear like she had a strange skin condition. She looked set for a night out on the town.

On the whole, Chris thought at first that she was hot, but looked 15. He wouldn't judge too quickly by pointing out that she resembled one of those girls who frequented the streets of Wan Chai on the weekends and most probably was a local at Fenwick's that he had brushed past several times.

Chris stumbled over his words as she sat down. She giggled continuously for the first few seconds, her left hand covered her soya-stained broken teeth. He sat smiling, but terrified inside. She looks like a kid, he said to himself. He asked her if she wanted a drink.

She nodded and said, 'A coffee.'

'Which kind?'

'Any kind, what kind do you like?' Her eyes tried to be seductive but failed to arouse any real interest in Chris.

'Me, umm, latte?'

'Okay, me too, I have latte too.' She grinned at him ferociously.

He nodded and walked to the counter with heavy legs as he already began to feel the strain from walking up those stairs. Waiting to order, he smiled at Candy from afar, and she waved back enthusiastically with her right hand, the left still covering her mouth, which remained in a fit of giggles.

Turning away from her, he hid the confused wrinkle on his forehead. He looked over at the Western girl with bad skin who sat with an air of sadness and loneliness. The girl felt him stare and brought her eyes toward him. Strangely, she held the stare, as if they had met, or at the very least had seen each other before. She gave him a slight smile. Chris, delighted, returned it, but then the girl's phone rang, and she became distracted, digging it out from the depths of her enormous bag. The blast from the froth machine hid her voice, but he thought he heard a name.

Finally, the girl behind the counter placed the latte down, calling him back to the moment and away from the girl's smile. Deep in concentration, he juggled some brown sugar sachets and thin wooden stirrers on top of the lid and moved back toward an elated Candy.

Putting the beverage down in front of her, he noticed that she quickly gasped at it with delight. Gently, she removed the lid and touched the white foam on the top with the thin wooden stick. She licked the foam from the stick, her eyes illuminated with mock surprise. 'Mmm.'

Chris smiled and began to start with the introduction he had practiced in the shower this morning and yesterday evening. He opened his mouth, ready to dive into his story when she squealed again into a fit of giggles resembling a starving piglet. He looked at her, shocked.

'What?' he asked.

She shook her head and slowly half pointed toward his stomach.

He immediately looked down, seeing the purple stain he hadn't caught. 'Oops.'

He tried to rub it out, but it got worse, and she giggled some more. He began to grow impatient when she declared very loudly, shaking her head, 'No, not that, that.' She pointed further at his stomach.

'What?' he replied, looking down again, feeling helpless.

'You are fat! You have big stomach!'

'What?' he whispered back, his face rising in warmth.

'Yes,' she nodded, still giggling, 'you are fat!'

Chris searched the room to see whether anyone else had heard their conversation. Thankfully, no one had. He returned to her in disbelief. 'I'm not fat,' he sputtered.

'Yes, you are fat!' she answered. Apparently, this was some cute game she liked to play. He was a little heavy, average by European standards; however, this often translated to obese in the East.

'Hmm,' he searched for a reply, 'yes, well…'

'You eat too much,' she announced triumphantly, provoking him with her flirty child eyes.

'You think?' he replied, lost. He had no idea what to say next. He tried to smile, but internally, he felt like the ice being torn apart in the blender.

'Yes, too much. You need eat less, no tummy, that is what I like.'

'Oh, okay,' he sounded relieved, finally able to change the subject. 'What else do you like?'

'Umm,' she grinned, 'I like coffee,' she said and pointed to the latte she had yet to really taste. 'I like making people happy. I like children.' Her words stumbled out poorly, like clogged water from a steamer. 'I like dancing!'

On this fact, she started to clap her hands. 'Would you like to see me dance?' she said, as she started to rise out of her chair.

Chris was quick to stop her, grabbing her little elbow tenderly.

He spoke softly, 'No, not now, later.'

She appeared falsely hurt and said, 'Okay.'

Finally, she picked up her oversized latte when Chris asked, 'Where do you come from?'

'Manila in the Philippines.'

'Oh, right.'

'Have you been there?' she asked, wide-eyed.

'No, not yet.' Chris shook his head. His brain began to realize that this wasn't such a good idea.

'Okay, it is not so nice. Lot people, lot cars.'

He continued, 'What do you do here?'

She looked at him confused.

He spoke slower, 'For a job — what do you do for work?'

'I work for nice lady. She come from Europe, like you — how do you say, Germland?'

'You mean Germany?' he replied.

'Yes, Germany.' she said, looking angry at him as if it was his fault he didn't understand her.

'What do you do for her?'

'I clean house and wash,' she said, and looked up as if she was searching for the word, 'I wash clothes.'

'Do you like it?'

'Yes,' she nodded with a shrug of the shoulders, 'it is okay, but I want to dance.'

'Oh, yes?'

'I am very good dancer. You will see!' she said, playfully nodding her head.

He smiled back politely and checked his fake Rolex.

She reacted quickly, sensing his disinterest. 'Chris,' her hand searched for his on the table. When she found it, she asked softly, 'Where you live?'

His hand was trapped, clinched in hers, and uncomfortably he answered, 'Happy Valley.'

'Yes, with the horses?' This caused her to giggle hysterically.

'Yes, with horses.'

'You live with horses.' More giggles.

Chris, bored, sighed. 'No, I live near the racetrack.'

Suddenly, the giggles died, and a serious wave swept over her young face. 'I want go there. No one take me. Will you take me?'

Chris looked down at his hand wishing that it were free, 'Yes, if you want.'

'You have a big apartment?'

'No, not very big.'

'How many bedroom have you?'

'Two.'

'Two rooms and just you?' she said, astonished.

Chris couldn't stand these questions. Nodding, he could no longer look at her face.

'Wow, that big. You rich!' She clapped down her hands on the table in amazement.

'No,' he shook his head, feeling his stomach begin to swell, 'not really.'

THE COFFEE SHOP MASQUERADE

'I would like to see your apartment. It nice, yes?' She continued, trying to entice him to embellish, but he couldn't and grew distant. She was acting like all the other girls he had met, and he began to resent her and his own stupidity in thinking she would be any different, but he looked at her eager eyes and felt that he couldn't take it out on her.

'Did you have many calls?'

'Calls?' she replied, confused.

'Yes,' showing his annoyance for the first time, mimicking a phone receiver, 'ring, ring, telephone calls.'

'Oh yes, many, many.' She dropped his hand and threw her hands up to exaggerate the number.

'Have you met many of the men?' Chris asked, curiously.

'Yes, I met all of them!' she answered, very blasé.

'All of them?' Chris now was surprised.

'Yes, many men, some old men, they were not so nice.'

'But the others? You like them?'

'Yes, of course.' she relayed in a normal tone.

'Oh.' Chris replied, defeated, yet unsurprised.

She smiled at him and pressed his hand. She said reassuringly, 'But you are also nice.'

'Thank you.' He pondered and looked outside the window. 'Candy, I want to ask you something.'

'Yes?' she giggled, anticipating a favorable question.

'Where did you get the word 'sincere' from?'

She blankly stared back at him and scrunched up her forehead.

"Sincere'?' Chris said loudly and slowly as he dug out the torn classified page from his shorts. He placed it on the table and pointed at the word, "Sincere.' Your ad—the word 'sincere."

Suddenly, the storeroom door creaked open wide, and most people who sat in the shop looked up, expecting someone to come out, but no one did. The girl who served Chris stared at the door curiously, walked over, and looked into the room. There was no one there, and she closed it again.

Chris returned to Candy's eyes. He repeated, "Sincere.' Your ad — the word 'sincere.''

'Oh, 'Sinceeere,'' she sang.

'No, 'sin-cere.' Where did it come from?'

'The dry cleaner's shop, next where I live. It called sincerrreee, I think it such pretty word. I ask German lady what it mean — she said it mean something nice, something true. The German lady, she help me writing this ad — she said she help me to find nice man, sinceeere man. She pay for the magazine, so I use it. I feel like I am nice and true also — you think so?'

Chris' hand fell from their embrace. It was now his turn to giggle continuously, but it turned into a deep laugh, forcing his eyes to stare up at the dusty ceiling fan rotating slowly. The storeroom door opened again.

Candy sat silently, she smiled trying to understand his private, silent joke. His insides shook as he realized his own ignorance. A dry cleaner's name held his private truth, this search for sincerity. He laughed because he couldn't sum up any other emotion. The others in the coffee shop looked over at his loud release of emotion, and a couple of them smiled out of embarrassment for Chris.

Candy's face began to fall when she realized the joke was on her. Chris stood up and bowed his head toward hers. He took hold of her small fingers and looked down at her tanned hand, so dark in its color compared with his own, and he gently pressed his lips on it. She smiled and stood up to go with him, assuming this joke was over.

'Thank you, Candy, but no thank you.' he said softly.

Her eyes followed him through the glass doors to the nearest taxi that sat waiting beside the escalator on Staunton Street. He jumped in, not looking back. He smiled the whole way home and decided to leave these girls alone and try his luck with others. He would ignore the wise words of his predecessor, who informed him that these girls were so easy, it was like picking up fallen apples off the floor. Obviously, it wasn't, and he didn't want to pretend anymore.

Perhaps that girl eating that muffin, maybe she would be interested, and he cursed out loud, thinking that he should've got her number. What was that name she said? He could barely hear it above the bloody cappuccino machine. Emma, Emily? But I don't know anyone named that. He asked the driver to turn around, but the driver spoke angrily into the wire that hung around his neck, and Chris left it alone, thinking that if it was right, he would see her again.

3

FRIENDS BY CIRCUMSTANCE

Those who know don't talk.
Those who talk don't know.
–Tao Te Ching

Emma and Sophia met last year in the bathroom of a nightclub. They had little in common apart from the fact that they were both foreigners, in their mid-twenties and that they were born on the 13th day of a month. Unlucky for some, some would say.

They sat side by side on the coffee shop's red couch, its filthy dark brown cushions stained with splashes of coffee and chocolate smudges. The crumbs of a two-day-old croissant lay trapped in between the cushions, invisible to those who sat above them.

Sophia, bored with talking began to read the back of the sweetener packet. She appeared older due to her heavily made-up face. As an eight-month-trained makeup artist in Brisbane, she'd applied for a job in Hong Kong after her boyfriend had left her for her best friend. It had come as a great surprise to her when the company emailed and interviewed her over Zoom, they said they liked her avant garde Eastern European-heavy style. She accepted a modest package with benefits and jumped at the chance to get away from home.

THE COFFEE SHOP MASQUERADE

Emma sat beside her, she was timid and unsure of herself. Her new bold designer frames hid the mascara that had fallen and embedded itself in the small creases under her eyes. Her skin was covered in small bumps that she hadn't been able to get rid of since puberty, but due to good foundation, supplied by Sophia, she'd cleverly concealed them. A thick expensive cream mask to hide her imperfections. She pushed her frames closer to her face, her eyes slightly red and swollen after last night's cryfest. Crying was the only thing that helped her sleep, exhausting and comforting her when she's in her bed alone.

Both their bodies appeared slightly swollen due to the processed food they often consumed. It had been cheaper to eat out most nights than purchase fresh food and eat at home. They normally didn't go a day without their sweetened coffees and double chocolate muffins, allowing them to remain indifferent to the excess sugar on their bodies.

Emma sighed. She secretly wished she had saved enough money for eye laser surgery when she'd had the chance, but that wasn't going to happen now. She was left with the burden of rent, as Alex, her local ex-boyfriend had decided to go back to live with his parents in Sha Tin where he spent most of his days and nights in the pool halls of Tsim Sha Tsui. Emma could barely afford a plane ticket home, but kept all this hidden, not wanting to admit defeat, especially to Sophia.

But when she was honest with herself at night, lying still, she stared up at the poorly textured artex ceiling in the apartment that hadn't been renovated in years and was serviced once a week by an invisible maid who washed the parquet floor, she felt like she had failed in coming out here. She cried deeply, thinking about her foolishness in following Alex here, believing that this would be the start of a life together. He had told her that it would be easy, fun, that she would love it. Hong Kong is what every city should be. She did love it until Alex started to spend more time in the pool halls and eventually stopped coming home at night. And although her job was good and the money okay, it was still far removed from where she wanted to be, of what was expected of her.

Emma remembered the guy she saw yesterday in the coffee shop — who smiled at her and the weird thing between him and that Filipina girl. She considered mentioning it to Sophia, but paused, knowing she would ridicule her.

The possible dialogue between them played itself out in her head like a familiar song: She already could hear Sophia say, 'Stay away from those guys, mate, they'll always go back to those sorts of girls. Then Sophia would ask whether the guy was hot, which he wasn't, but Emma would say, 'He had kind eyes,' and Sophia would laugh, just as she laughed when Emma explained why she spent most of the night at Dragon Fly talking to a large Indian doctor. 'He was a nice guy who had volunteered at an orphanage for a year.' Sophia burst into cackling hysterics when she heard that, telling Emma she was too much of a pushover and how they always say stuff like that to get you into bed. Sophia then went on to explain in detail how she had spent the night with a Romanian model who had been drop-dead gorgeous, but was only in Hong Kong for a day, leaving Emma feeling as empty as the reality of Sophia's bed.

Emma glanced down at the cover of a magazine voted the best in Hong Kong, five years running. She smirked at the image of a skinny Asian woman dressed in Dior, her face painted in couture make up. She kneeled, her hands clasping onto a pear, her expression trying to be one of serenity, but it came across as silly, almost animated. The pear was the only decent thing in the picture, thought Emma, its skin perfectly illuminated. They would be better off going to the art galleries, Emma surmised, watching the colors and moods align, then collapse. That's where inspiration lies, not in these printed, glossy pages.

Easy-listening classical music filled the coffee shop, but it failed to remove the constant murmur from the air conditioning and the random splashes and spurts from the coffee machine. It was early afternoon, and lunchtime had been quiet.

Suddenly, the main door opened, and Sophia sat up straight, her neck regal like that of a trained bird. She nudged Emma and pointed carefully at the door, and they both began to laugh, the knowing laugh of a private joke shared with two.

A tall older Western woman walked in. She was oddly dressed, with a deep flowing purple skirt and a well-worn denim jacket. Her ash-colored hair was in messy braids, and the crown of her head was greasy. A necklace of various keys and beads laced her neck. Her clothes were just as oily, dotted with erratic splotches of bleach, but to some observers, they resembled one of those modern designs of fabric filled with contrasting runs of stains.

The woman fixed her eyes on the menu above the barista's face while letting her body gently sway to the music. The barista looked upon her with ease, obviously used to her presence. She never ordered anything and normally would depart abruptly, mumbling quiet obscenities. It no longer embarrassed him, so he kept a mildly attentive eye on her while he rearranged the lineup of muffins.

She was one of the twins. Apparently, there were two of them, but they rarely were seen together. They were once very prominent Western socialites in their heyday, yet for some forgotten reason, both had fallen from grace. They both were in their early 60s, although it was hard to tell under their long gray hair and blank eyes. These once beautiful women had become reliant on drugs, or so it was said. Stories circulated that they were involved with the Triads or that they had shared the same rich local husband, and that he could no longer put up with their jealousy for each other and left in the middle of the night, fleeing back to the mainland. Both women blamed the other and would cause a disturbance every time they would see each other wandering the streets of Soho or Lan Kwai Fong.

The woman looked down at the barista, suddenly sensing that she was at the center of people's attention. She swore under her breath and ran out of the coffee shop in a frenzied whirlwind, knocking over the stand of various African coffee packets. The barista sighed, and in his native tongue, motioned for his two subordinates to pick them up.

Sophia and Emma roared with laughter.

'What a freak!' Sophia announced, her Australian accent quick to project in volume.

'Yeah, I know, but it's sort of sad.' Emma looked at the door as her laughter stopped fast, leaving her with empathy. She didn't like the vicious way in which Sophia always made things out to be so harsh. Emma thought there was always something at the core of weird behavior, some trauma, people weren't strange for no reason, which she secretly attributed to her being better educated than Sophia, but she would never tell her that.

Emma once admitted to Alex that the only reason she was friends with Sophia was because they were similar in age and, well, because she was lonely. Sophia was the only person who wanted to see her more than once a month. 'Everyone is so busy,' she had said, and it was easy being with Sophia. 'She talks crap, but at least she wants to go out.'

'Yeah, yeah, whatever,' Sophia said and looked around at the Coffee Shop's interior. 'Maybe she was wise to go. This place sucks, the coffee is crap, the service is awful, and they have the worst cake! You can just taste the starch and preservatives in this.' She motioned at the half brownie, its other side consumed, leaving a trail of tiny brown crumbs lying on her top. 'And you know what's worse? This place is more expensive than Starbucks! Why are we even here?' Sophia flicked her hair in defiance and folded her arms.

Emma admired her dramatic stance. She certainly did grab others' attention, but as there was no one else in the vicinity, her performance fell flat on Emma.

'Because we can never get a seat in Starbucks,' Emma replied, softly keeping her English accent together. It had become apparent to Emma that the Australian accent was too easy to copy. Sometimes she would come home, and Alex would laugh at her new tongue. 'You're always complaining about the guy who works there who is constantly watching you.'

Sophia smiled, 'Yeah, I know, but hey, at least we get free muffins!'

'Yeah, but no one comes here, and at least we can have a seat.'

'Hmm, a shitty seat.'

'Well, why don't we just go?' Emma said, reaching for her bag.

Sophia retracted 'No, no, it's fine, that guy in Starbucks is beginning to freak me out a bit. I forgot to tell you he, like, knows my name now.'

'How?'

'Last week, you know we had that Sun Beach promo party?'

Emma scrunched her eyes, trying to remember.

'You know, the one you couldn't go to?' Sophia continued.

Emma nodded quickly.

'Well, they made us wear name badges. I hadn't eaten all day, and I was starving, so I went down to get a sandwich and totally forgot to take off my name tag.'

'Oh,' Emma bit her lip, 'and he saw it?'

'Yeah, totally. He kept saying my name, 'Hi, Sophia. What else would you like Sophia? Isn't that a pretty name, Sophia?' and when I left, he said, 'Please come again, Sophia.' Ugh, it was so embarrassing, and there was, like, all these amazing, gorgeous guys in there.'

'Really? Wow,' Emma said subdued, for wherever Sophia went, there always appeared to be amazing, gorgeous guys.

'Anyway, I can't believe you didn't come to that promo thing,' she said, then gently hit Emma on the arm. 'It was so cool. I did the makeup on these two anorexic Chinese models, and they had the worst skin ever. It was awful,' Sophia relayed, excitedly.

Emma, feeling the shame of her own troubled skin, pulled her bag closer to her chest. 'How did they look?'

'Okay, I did my best, but makeup can only help so much. I told them to have surgery or take some medication for it or something.'

'You didn't!' Emma said, amused. It made her feel good that Sophia hardly ever mentioned her own skin problems, and she found comfort in knowing that Sophia believed that there was someone else out there with worse problems than her own.

'Yeah, they looked bad, and to be honest, they already had cellulite coming on. The company must have got them for free or something. Martin threw a fit!' Sophia said, biting the remains of her middle fingernail.

Then the main door was pushed open, and a flood of hot air came through relieving the coldness in the shop. Sophia, always attentive in the presence of men, automatically sat up.

Emma continued, oblivious to the change in Sophia. 'I'm sorry I missed it. It was that day I was waiting for my test results.'

Sophia grabbed Emma's hand hard. 'I know that guy!'

Emma looked over at the guy who stood staring confusingly

at the menu. He was tall and brown. Okay-looking, she thought. Kind of nondescript, one of the many words she had absorbed from Sophia.

'He's, like, friends with Dave.' Sophia moved excitedly and checked her hair. 'Oh my god. I don't want him to see me. I look awful. Ugh, is he looking?'

Emma looked over and suddenly felt sorry for this guy with no name. There he was, happily ordering a long black, innocent to the drama that his entrance had caused. Emma wondered how interested he would really be in Sophia's flirting technique, but then she sat back, remembering the enjoyment she felt watching Sophia at work. She was excellent at devouring men and making them squirm, especially when there was another woman around.

'God, he's hot! Don't you think he's hot?' Sophia asked, not wanting a reply.

'Not especially.'

'Okay, are you mad?' Sophia turned her body to face Emma. Immediately, her voice rose up a notch—not too much for the guy with no name to understand what she was saying, but for him to at least look over and notice his native tongue. Emma looked at her and sat further into the couch, waiting for Sophia's next move.

Sophia said, 'Dave said that he was asked to be a surfer model for Billabong in Brisbane or something.'

Emma nodded without enthusiasm. According to Sophia, it seemed like everyone in Australia was a model for something.

'Yeah, he's hot,' Sophia looked wistfully over at him. 'Shit, he saw me.'

The guy with no name tilted his head back in recognition of Sophia. He picked up his long black to go and walked over to the small steps toward the red couch. He was confident, but as he reached the other end, he realized that no one else was sitting up there, and he immediately became insecure. He didn't even remember this girl's name.

'Hi there.' he said.

'Hi, how's it going?' Sophia sat up, acting casual.

He stared at her, trying desperately to remember her. Was it last Friday at the Australian Association thing? Suddenly, it washed over him — she was Dave's ex, 'Sara ... Sara, right?'

'Yeah, close enough — Sophia.' she replied, not at all fazed that he didn't remember her name.

'Yeah, of course. How's it going?'

'Good, yeah, you know, and you? What are you doing here?'

The guy with no name stared down at the two smiling faces. 'What, here? I'm ordering coffee.'

Sophia playfully rolled her eyes. 'No, not here silly, in Hong Kong.'

'Oh right, gotcha. I'm moving here. I'm in training to become a pilot with Cathay.'

'Oh, really? Can you get me some free flights?'

He smirked and fought the urge to roll his eyes. 'Maybe...'

Sophia laughed too loudly and looked over at Emma with open eyes for help. Emma smiled back from the safety of the couch and her own luck at being an observer of this awkward encounter. She was enjoying this, as she secretly liked feeling the tense silence between strangers.

The guy with no name searched his brain for something to say, but he had been caught off guard. He had just awakened half an hour ago after a big night out in Wan Chai with his cousin and had a pile of name cards in his pocket that he wanted to go home to and search through to find that Thai girl's number.

He continued, unaware of what he was saying: 'So, I heard you split up with Dave?'

'Yeah,' Sophia answered, shocked, but not giving up her

confidence. 'Wow, you get straight to the point.'

Now embarrassed and cursing himself for needing coffee, he replied, 'Yeah, well, it's what I heard.'

Sophia reacted swiftly, excellently displaying her lack of interest in the whole thing. 'Yeah, well, we couldn't do the whole long-distance thing. It wasn't really our style.'

He nodded. 'Yeah, right.' He then remembered seeing Dave last month at a beach party with a beautiful brunette. 'Yeah, of course,' he replied, then exhaled and sighed. 'I better be off, girls. It was nice to see you both. I have an appointment,' he quickly said and continued to embellish the lie. 'I'm looking for an apartment.'

Sophia perked up, 'Cool, where you looking?'

'Mid-Levels, Wan Chai, you know, the usual.'

'Cool, yeah.'

He felt the coffee emitting warmth around his fingers, and it suddenly made him feel tired. He then escaped her stare and looked down at the floor. 'I guess I better go. I'll see you around then.'

Sophia gave him her best flirty eyes, 'Yeah, sure.' As he turned and swiftly walked away, she called back after him, making him stop and turn, 'Oh, hey, good luck.'

'Thanks.' he replied and rushed out.

Sophia turned to Emma, 'Oh my god, he's so hot! Wow, I think I really like him!'

Emma turned up her lips, sensing that this guy didn't have any feelings for her. 'Really?'

'Do you think he likes me?'

Emma nodded, biting her upper lip, 'Of course.'

'Wow, yeah, and you see how he mentioned Dave — he knows I'm available and wants me.'

Emma nodded and stared transfixed at the magazine to try

and shield her face as she smothered laughter.

Sophia looked up helplessly toward the door. 'Shit, I should've given him my number. Fuck, he was so hot.'

Emma, unable to hide anymore, picked up the magazine and opened it to a page filled with local Hong Kongians whom she didn't recognize and answered with a muffled, 'Yeah, I know.'

Sophia, unable to let go, said, 'Maybe I should go and catch up with him. Hold on, okay?'

Emma's amusement stopped, and she lowered the magazine. 'Are you serious? What about what you said yesterday?'

'What?'

'About letting things happen naturally?'

'Yeah, well, I did, just forgot to give him my number. Oh, come on, man, don't make that face. He was so hot! Won't be two secs.' Sophia and her self-confidence rushed out of the coffee shop.

Emma grabbed her phone and unlocked it—no missed calls. Feeling she had reached her quota of Sophia for the day; she racked her brain trying to think of someone to call—someone who wouldn't answer but would have to call her back—then she could excuse herself and be able to leave Sophia's clutches safely. She looked at the time. It was 9:30 a.m. in England on a Monday, so her mom would be out getting her hair done, then she could call her back. She rang and left a quick message on the phone.

Sophia returned, beaded with sweat. Emma quickly put away her phone. Sophia collapsed back into the couch, seemingly exhausted.

'Well, did you catch him?' Emma asked.

'No,' Sophia sighed, staring at her tight belt. 'He disappeared.'

'I'm sure you'll see him again.'

Annoyed, Sophia kicked the soiled napkin on the floor, 'Yeah, fuck! I guess so.' She then sat up fast, refueled with a thought,

'We're soooo going out on Friday night.'

Emma looked anxiously at her. 'No, I can't. I have a dinner thing.'

'What dinner thing?' Sophia demanded.

'A work thing.' Emma remained vague, not really wanting to embellish on the fact that her work colleague's boyfriend had managed to get a table at the China Club.

'Oh, well,' Sophia said. 'What time does it finish?'

'I don't know.'

'Well, you can't abandon me this Friday. I need you, mate, more than ever.' Sophia then looked at her, hurt and determined.

Emma raised her eyebrows. Suddenly, she had enough of Sophia manipulating her and spoke in her well-paid accent, 'I'm hardly abandoning you.' She searched her brain for a solution, 'Why not go out with your roommate?'

Sophia stared at her in disbelief. 'What, Michelle? No fucking way, and watch her and her mates iron their way through the evening? Are you joking?'

Emma sighed heavily and replied quietly to her crudeness with an air of superiority. 'You know,' she said, staring down at her hands, 'you don't have to snort cocaine if you don't want to.'

She looked up to meet Sophia's eyes, saw their offense, and offered her a playful smile.

Sophia put up her right hand, 'Yeah, okay mate, whatever you think.'

Lowering her hand, Sophia bit down on her perfectly shaded lip. Emma felt the change and became aware that she was fighting off tears. Often, they would come out, and Sophia would sit there and let them fall, not saying anything.

Emma had heard her story several times — the lesbian mother and the drunken father. Initially, it had been a sad story, but now, it had escalated into the ridiculous, with her mother leaving her girlfriend for another woman, some prison guard, and the father getting arrested for wearing no clothes in the supermarket. Emma wondered whether these parents really existed or if Sophia was just trying to cover the fact that they were ordinary people living very normal lives. It made her feel uneasy when Sophia cried; she found it hard to believe her sadness or remorse. Thankfully, the tears didn't come now.

Sophia said quietly, 'Yeah, whatever mate, I'll be the sober one in the corner, which will be fun.'

Looking over at Emma, Sophia continued with residues of forced politeness, feeling Emma's apprehension said, 'can't you get out of the dinner thing?'

Emma looked down at her bag, contemplating whether to take it and her phone to the bathroom, ring her neighbor, and ask her to call her back so she would have an excuse to leave this draining situation. 'No, I can't. It's important.'

'Great!' Sophia returned and sank back into the red couch.

A waitress walked toward them dressed in a red apron and black trousers with a tray and a cloth.

Emma read her name tag, 'Jasmine.' She thought, wow, she's so pretty, her eyes.

Sophia tutted and shook her head. 'Umm, we're not finished.'

Jasmine looked at her blankly, and she signaled cleaning.

Sophia used her hands to signal a cross of the fingers.

'No,' she said as she shook her head and spoke slowly, 'not finished.'

Jasmine walked away confused. There were empty cups, and all that remained was a pile of crumbles and half a brownie on the red-glazed chipped plate.

'Fucking hell,' Sophia cursed, growing back into herself, 'what bad service.'

She looked over at Emma, who hadn't acknowledged the

episode and continually stared at her phone, quietly wishing for it to ring.

Sophia relaxed her anger and tried to bring Emma back, 'So, what are you doing tonight?'

Emma muttered, 'Gym and then sleep.' She forgot the phone and looked at Sophia's face and said, 'I need to catch up on sleep; it's been a bit too party-party recently.'

Sophia nodded, 'I know what you mean. I got, like, two hours on Sunday, four hours on Monday, and, like, one hour last night. I just can't sleep. I'm a total insomniac.' She waited for looks of concern to come flooding out from Emma, but all she got was a sigh. Sophia continued, saying quickly, 'Michelle's seeing this Indian guy who keeps smoking dope and listening to reggae.' Her thoughts took over her speech, 'God, she's so pathetic. Do you know she has, like, two full fat thighs? Pure cellulite.'

Emma picked up on this bitchy piece of information and sat up, turning herself toward Sophia. She took pleasure in gory pieces of bitchiness; it always helped mask her own deficiencies. Sophia, now fueled by the attention, continued as she leaned in and spoke softly so as not to disturb the empty room. Emma leaned in toward her.

'It's all the cocaine and drinking. She also eats the worst food, all delivery. She'd better be careful or else no one's going to want her.'

Emma nodded, then a vision of Michelle and the photo she had taken of her last weekend before they went out entered her mind. 'She's okay, Sophia. She's quite pretty.'

'Yeah,' Sophia persisted, 'but only when I put a ton of makeup on her. She's a total control freak, mate. You know her moods. Fuck, even I'm scared of her.' She laughed out loud, self-consciously.

Emma's thoughts returned to her wish for a phone call, as she already had been inundated by these stories of Michelle's moods and Sophia's hardships. She was fed up with the moaning and complaining. Suddenly, the jazz music picked up, with loud beats bubbling with happy lyrics. It annoyed her and encouraged her to ask with a playful harshness, 'Why don't you move out?'

Sophia reacted, offended, 'You know I can't. Jeez, mate, what's up with you today?'

Emma stared at the entrance, blocking out Sophia's comment as a familiar acquaintance of theirs walked in.

Emma panicked inside. 'Oh shit,' she said as she sank back into the red couch, 'there's Needlam.'

Sophia stood up, staring frantically at the familiar dark hair, secretly amused by Emma's change. 'Where? Oh yeah.' She smiled, falling back onto the couch.

'Oh my god, I'm so embarrassed.' Emma searched for a pillow to hide herself behind.

'Shit,' Sophia said, 'well, let me do the talking.'

Needlam, after finishing her order, caught Sophia's eyes and waved at her. She tottered over toward the two in her high-heeled sandals, unaware that she had imposed on their secret inferior hideaway. She smiled, happily clutching onto her new Vuitton purse. 'Hey, guys!' she said, searching their faces.

'Hey, honey!' Sophia replied, standing up to air-kiss her. Emma stood up, nervous, and greeted her.

'Good to see you both,' said Needlam. 'What's happening?' She quickly looked down at the table, which was flooded with last month's magazines and two empty cups.

'Nothing much,' Sophia grinned, 'just catching up.'

Needlam smiled sweetly. 'Well,' she looked at Emma, 'you look in better shape than the last time I saw you.'

Emma forced a smile, and Sophia giggled.

Needlam continued: 'You were a complete riot at my party.'

Emma looked down, embarrassed, and said nothing. 'But you left so early.'

'Yeah, well, I was pretty drunk,' Emma said, trying desperately hard to appear relaxed about the whole thing. Her good manners got the better of her, as she added, 'I'm so sorry if I embarrassed you.'

'No,' Needlam answered, surprised, 'not at all! Everyone loved you, especially when you started to sing 'Happy Birthday' to the waiter.'

Emma then turned the same shade of red as the couch as she stared into Needlam's dark eyes. Sheepishly, she uttered, 'I did, really? I'm sorry.'

Needlam laughed, 'Hey, no worries. It was hilarious.'

Emma felt worse and decided that she couldn't associate with this crowd anymore. She had stupidly overstepped her mark and would be known eternally as the girl who got drunk and sang 'Happy Birthday' to the waiter. She knew this type of crowd; they were similar to the one she had grown up with, and she knew how far you could go before you were made a mockery, and too much champagne had placed her over that limit.

Needlam, comfortable with her hold over Emma, decided to change the subject to an area she felt very powerful with. 'So,' she asked, trying not to appear showy, 'you guys going to the Armani party on Saturday?'

Sophia immediately sat up, resembling a dog that had been called by her master. 'Umm,' she placed her lips together. 'Maybe. I haven't managed to snag any tickets. Are you?'

'Of course,' Needlam said, slightly offended that she even had to be asked. She noticed the droop in Sophia's expression and felt a twinge of guilt for a moment.

'Let me have a chat with Navin,' she offered, 'he might be able to get some for you.'

Sophia smiled at her with eyes filled with hope. Needlam felt good about her apparent charity, though normally, when she left these situations, she would forget her kind offer and never follow up.

'Really?' Sophia said excitingly, 'that would be amazing.'

'Of course,' Needlam reassured with good favor. 'It's going to be pretty cool. Everyone will be there.' Sophia nodded enthusiastically as Emma looked on with hopeful eyes. Needlam's memory jolted into gear as she looked down and admired Emma's oversize Tod's bag.

'Oh, Emma, I was going to ask you about those shoes you were wearing to my party. You said they were Gucci?' Emma's eyes expanded, trying hard to think of which pair she was referring to; she didn't own a pair of Gucci shoes.

'Oh, those.' Emma realized and began to burn again with red tints lining her neck.

'Did you get them here?' Needlam inquired.

Emma searched her imagination and cursed herself for ever drinking a drop of alcohol.

'No,' she gently cleared her throat, 'I bought them in London last year.'

Needlam sighed. 'Oh, I thought so. Europe always gets the best from the collections. They were so gorgeous,' she said truthfully. 'Everyone was talking about them at the party.' And then Needlam said something she rarely admitted to anyone except herself sometimes, 'You know you have great taste.'

Emma, unaware of the magnitude of the sentence coming from Needlam, smiled slightly and uttered a timid 'Thanks.'

'Well,' Needlam said, turning her head to see the increasing line at the counter, 'I better go. I actually can't believe I'm here. You know yesterday, I used the bathroom here, and I heard someone crying. I came out and told the staff, and they said there was no one in there except me. So weird.' Her eyes wandered over the shabby décor, and she said, 'This place is definitely haunted, but at least it's quicker than standing in line in Starbucks. Anyway!' Her hands motioned for the goodbye insincerity kiss. Sophia stood up and acted her role.

'Give me a call,' Needlam said with airs of pretend concern. She then moved to Emma and acted the same role. 'Bye,' she said and floated down to the counter to pick up her still-steaming hot Americano.

Emma sat back in the couch and announced, 'God, that was embarrassing.' She leaned forward and placed her hands on the top of her head, trying to talk herself out of being sick.

Sophia picked up and played with the plastic wrapper from yesterday's cake. 'Why?' she said, 'I told you that you were a dickhead at that party.'

Emma shot her a mean glance and pointed to the door, 'Well, she didn't seem to think so.'

Sophia ignored the mean glance and replied, 'Yeah, but she's being polite — that's what she does for a living.'

Emma felt hurt, and her rage at Sophia overshadowed her embarrassment, but the humiliation, thicker in its grip, returned, forcing her to fall back rapidly into the sick pose.

'I knew I shouldn't have gone,' she cursed herself.

Sophia muttered, 'Yeah, well.'

Emma heard her brushing crumbs off her nylon top. She crossed her hands and let them carry the weight of her head, then she gave out a small laugh from a memory. 'You know what's funny though?' she said, looking at Sophia, her eyes blinking from the adjustment to the change of the light. Sophia, busy with crumbs, acknowledged her eyes.

'You know my supposedly Gucci shoes?'

Sophia stopped with the brushing.

Emma bent in toward her and said softly, 'I bought them in Shenzhen for $50.'

Sophia laughed out loud, 'What? And you said they were from Gucci?'

'I was drunk—I couldn't let myself down.' Emma grinned.

'Wow, and Needlam believed you? She works for Vuitton. Of course she might have been testing you,' Sophia said negatively and provokingly.

Emma relaxed back into the funniness of it and sighed, 'Oh God, who cares. It's all shit talk anyway!'

Sophia looked toward the door and froze as Emma once more reached for her bag, then violently latched onto Emma's arm. 'Oh my god,' she said, 'did you see that guy?'

Emma sighed and was about to reiterate some plea about letting go of these guys, but then she saw Sophia's face. She looked happy, so she rotated her head toward the door. 'Where?'

'He just walked out.' Sophia stood up with a clear mission. 'He's heading down toward your gym. Let's go! Hurry up!'

'What? Oh Sophia, what the hell?' Emma said, praying for her phone to ring again. It was going to be another one of those days spent with Sophia, wasting their one day off, running all over town, drinking coffee and eating crap pretending they were 15 again, when they were hiding from 30.

'Come on, he's totally hot!'

The male barista cautiously walked over to them again as they picked up their bags with speed.

'Sorry, ladies,' he said, aware that apologizes are always a good start, 'Could you fill out this questionnaire?'

Emma looked at him and said politely, 'What's it about?'

'No! Come on!' Sophia said, gripping hold of her arm tightly as she jumped up and down to see where this vision of a man was going.

THE COFFEE SHOP MASQUERADE

The barista ignored Sophia and stared into Emma's eyes. 'It's about the coffee shop.'

Sophia, now fully impatient, tugged at Emma and dragged her toward the door. 'It's crap, okay?' she said too loudly, capturing the attention of fellow coffee drinkers, who stared at her.

'Come on!' As they reached the door, Emma looked back at the barista who stared at them, he held onto a piece of paper filled with boxes and mouthed a 'Sorry.'

They rushed out, causing four taxis to honk angrily as they ran across a busy Staunton Street. They stopped fast when they saw him sitting on the concrete steps outside the gym, consumed with his phone.

Sophia pointed excitedly and whispered, 'That's him.'

Emma stared at this guy, who was wearing a tanned leather headband, gladiator sandals, and a white kaftan top. She asked confused, 'What? Him? He looks like Jesus.'

'Yeah,' Sophia said as her eyes expanded, 'a hot Jesus!'

They both giggled loudly, as they considered this the best way to grab his attention. Then suddenly, a lone shoe fell right in front of them. They stopped and looked up.

'What the hell?' Sophia said.

'You know I've seen so many random shoes around here during the last few days. All different colors and styles. Like someone is making a trail.'

'Who would throw down a shoe?'

'I have no idea.' Emma kept looking up, and for a moment thought she saw a large animal on the roof of the gym staring down at her.

Sophia grabbed hold of her arm. 'Come on, maybe Jesus can tell us about the shoes.'

Emma's phone rang in her bag. It was her mother thousands of miles away returning her call, but she didn't hear it above their laughter. She looped her arm around Sophia's, preparing to walk over to ask 'Hot Jesus' the time.

Rush hour had started, and the mechanical stairs were crammed full of people with tired eyes their ears covered by headphones.

Lucy, the madwoman, walked past them, irritated at their laughter, and their volume increased as they saw her again.

'Like a batch of silly hens,' she shouted over to them, midway through a thought.

'Whatever, crazy lady.' Sophia said, shooing her away. She then turned her eyes to the hot guy, 'Hello there, you must be Jesus.'

Monkey sat above them on the roof, confused. He was in the middle of throwing out his old shoes, but his hearing was excellent, he looked carefully over the edge. Did she say Jesus? Like the white man's god?

4

Mad Lucy

Courage to dare kills,
Courage not to dare saves.
−Tao Te Ching

Lucy had been in a cycle of shame for over 50 years. Suppressed deep shame over what had happened to her as a child that she had never articulated to anyone. She didn't have any friends and rarely spoke to people. She walked around life mimicking villains from old cartoon shows that she loved as a child — caricatures of mean people who were despised or ridiculed, like Gargamel from 'The Smurfs' and 'Scooby Doo' baddies.

'It is better to be feared,' her father would say late at night to her, 'than "liked."'

Today she struggled lifting a heavy plastic bag up onto her old cracked pink kitchen counter, her arms ached as she let it go, its contents an assortment of bottles filled with toxic disinfectants and bleaches.

Sighing, she realized that she'd forgotten to purchase latex gloves. She stared down at her stinging hands, their dermis now thin in reaction to the various toxic cleaners she used, like saltwater eroding limestone, they felt sore and weak.

As she unpacked the plastic bottles from the bags, she also

realized she'd forgotten to buy another brush and mop head. The old ones were now no longer safe, as she'd stupidly let them dry on the communal staircase, and when she'd gone to retrieve them, she could smell a hint of cat urine and immediately stopped using the small narrow space, leaving them to ferment forever on the concrete stairs. She scanned the kitchen for a scrap of paper to scribble down the items she'd forgotten to buy, her thoughts turned to those human obstacles who'd distracted her during her early morning shopping—*those bloody women and children*, she thought, brooding.

Upon noticing the old newspaper article attached to her refrigerator door that detailed the warning signs of COVID-19, she removed it carefully and immediately started to write small and messily on the clear header underneath the old date. Lucy's mind grew distracted as it started to twitch in volatile thoughts: They shouldn't be allowed to bring those monsters into the shop. If it hadn't been for that little brat running around—mixed breed he was too—I'd have remembered to get the brushes, confusing me with his squeal like a little pig. And that thing running after him, well, she soon picked up her speed when she saw me, didn't she. Little monster. What did she expect, that I'd kiss that thing? The germs that must live on that!

Lucy soon forgot that thought when she noticed the wording on the shop's signature plastic bag. There had been a pitiful injection of some Christmas mistletoe that wound itself throughout the plain solid blue lettering in a lavish attempt to produce a more festive appeal. She glowered at it in distaste. What a waste of money! It's only packaging. Didn't these companies have better things to spend their money on? She took this little piece of festive labelling personally, another reminder of this foolish season. She sighed deeply and shook her head. It was one of the last festive bags of the season. They soon would return to their standard images.

Christmas and New Year's had come and gone, and Lucy had stayed far away from well-wishers and marketing ploys to make you spend more, spending that time inside, in the darkness, away from the false Christmas cheer that soaked the city in flashing fairy lights and cardboard cut-outs of snowmen and elves. Many local people viewed it as a normal day and went about their lives as if nothing was happening behind the walls of the high-rise apartments where Westerners sat huddled in their endeavors to celebrate the season, filling their rooms with expensive electronic gifts and designer labels.

Lucy had noticed that the decorations were still up this morning, and she felt like writing to the council to complain. After all, didn't they know it was bad luck?

Yes, she reflected, that will get them going, say it's bad luck — that's all they're obsessed with anyway. Well, at least I should be able to get some good bargains at the supermarkets at the end of the month. They always seem to manage to reduce their overpriced items slightly, so she added more cleaning items to her list.

She clapped her left hand on her head and muttered a 'sweet Jesus' under her breath. She had thrown all the ads, including sales fliers, that had littered her mat early this morning out of the window. From her 60th floor apartment, they had fallen like gentle ripe petals, the wind blew them across the lobby toward the communal pool, where most of them landed softly. They floated in the pool, promoting their discounts to the sky. Lucy walked over to the window, opened it slightly, and stuck her head out to try and see whether she could retrieve them, but all she saw was a gardener trying to fish them out.

She had shrieked at the security guard on her way to the shop this morning about them.

'Lazy, lazy rat,' she had called him, while shaking her wooden cane at him. Hadn't he remembered that she didn't want to receive such glossy ads? She had awakened today to a brisk knock at the door, and upon opening it, she found a huge pile of them staring up at her.

She had grabbed some of them and carried them to her opened window. She had pushed them through the small opening and watched them float down. The rest she struggled to lift up, but she managed and went downstairs immediately, the elevator floors' descending numbers and mirrored doors encouraged her rage — everything took so long. She had thrown the heavy pile of them at the first security guard she saw.

'I instructed you a week ago that I didn't want these.'

The security man had stared blankly at her and looked down with embarrassment when an elderly couple stepped out of the lift. He had tried to assure her quietly that it hadn't been done on purpose, but she barked back at him, 'Lazy, lazy pig.'

He had persisted in trying to explain that it hadn't been him that she had dealt with, but another security man who forgot to pass on the message.

She had brushed off that claim with an unnecessarily rude comment: 'Well, what do you expect—you are all so imcompetent.' It was something her father would've said, something to put them in their place. Lucy had pointed at him with her cane, 'You'd better remember now, lazy pig, and you must show respect,' she commanded.

The security man had nodded. He had considered mentioning that those ads normally never get delivered direct to tenants' doors, and that the delivery boys weren't even allowed to enter the building. Most come through the post and were deposited into her thin aluminum mailbox. It must be one of her neighbors, he thought, or one of the kids, and he turned away from her, concealing his enjoyment at this childish prank. His supervisor then walked in, and Lucy had proceeded to continue expanding on the story of pure insolence. The supervisor had nodded and kindly directed her from the lobby to the stairs leading to Robinson Road.

'Would you like a taxi, Miss Lucy?' said one of the younger doormen, holding the glass door open for her.

'What! What do I want a taxi for? Do you think I'm made of money?'

She banged down her cane against the pavement. Immediately she had turned, ready to continue her rant, but stopped when she saw that the supervisor had disappeared quickly back into his office.

She swore under her breath. Pushed out into the day without a plan, she was furious but decided to go for a short walk. She hobbled over to the traffic lights. A group of schoolchildren stood on the opposite side, and Lucy greeted them with the look of war. The light turned green, and she shuffled, her back overtly slouched. The cane wasn't for any serious condition, but after she found it lying in one of the skips down on Stubbs Road, she had decided to use it, believing that people normally left you alone when you had a cane in this city, as they were too afraid to meet the eyes of an elderly person who might need assistance. Thus, she decided to play the part, along with that of the evil witch who built the candy-covered house in the classic tale. She had always wanted to be a mean old person, someone bitter and annoyed like her grandmother—noticing how everyone respected her and jumped whenever she said anything. Lucy's well-worn black smock dress with a dirt-encrusted dark-green cardigan contrasted greatly with the brightness of the day. Her ash hair appeared alive, looking as if she had forgotten to brush it for the past week, but it had been longer.

The local schoolchildren stared at her in amazement as they passed her, some with open mouths, some nervous with giggles. She quietly roared at them, hobbling over to the small hill. They whispered about her, some insinuated that she was a witch, some forgotten old teacher at Hogwarts, but their pale, tired-looking teacher calmed down their imaginations and had started to sing softly, 'Row, row, row your boat...' to distract their young minds.

Lucy sat down on one of the entrance walls outside the newly developed apartment block. She liked to sit there and gawk at the glossy cars and marvel at how many different shades of beige car designers could find. Steadily she watched the stream of morning late rush-hour traffic, she stared into the windows of every car and monitored for any face she could terrorize with her growl. Her eyes squinted in the sunshine of the day as she lifted her cane up to greet the many cars passing. She cursed their choice of vehicle and stares through quiet chanting whispers. Most of these commuters were used to her and ignored her nest of white hair. However, occasionally there was one child sitting in the back of the car marveling at the great apartments in the sky when Lucy would catch their eye and perform her witchery curse with the skinny cane. Often this provoked the innocent victim to cry, and a parent would lower the window and swear at Lucy. She would brush off their comments with her hands as if she was brushing away fallen breadcrumbs. The lights always changed fast, so this odd occurrence never lasted long. She then decided to get up and go to the supermarket and stock up on cleaning supplies.

In the kitchen, Lucy put away the bleaches and detergents, she wasn't in the mood to terrorize anymore children today — she was still upset over the lost ads and the deals she could be missing out on. She sighed and reminisced she had used to love Christmas, but that was a million years ago before everything happened—before her family settled here, her father died, and her sister moved to Australia.

Lucy shut her eyes tight, trying to stop the surges of memories that came out fast. They made her feel trapped, like the cigarette butts deeply trapped within the small grooves of the cobblestones beneath her. These memories kept her down long enough that she couldn't vacate her apartment for weeks, leaving her to dwell and sit in a state of panic. Brushing away the past, she took to rinsing the walls in chemical showers, washing away the germs and her memories as she swayed in the dark. Small triggers led to her destructive behavior.

But that was over for now. She had just come out of one of those episodes only a week ago and had no intention of returning to bleaching the walls. The supplies she purchased were in case there was another pandemic in Hong Kong.

She had considered moving; she had money. That was the main reason why the apartment building's supervisors and staff put up with her. Her father had designed the building in which she was living and most of the other Mid-Levels buildings, and when he died, he left her more than her sister after becoming infuriated at her for marrying an Australian.

'Destroying her purity with that of a scummy convict.' Lucy had recalled him saying that while sitting on her bed late one night stroking her left breast.

She tried to give her sister some of the money after time had passed, but she didn't want it, nor anything else that had to do with her, so Lucy left her alone after she hurled a blue Delft plate at her at the Ritz. They hadn't spoken to each other in years, and although her sister had moved back to Hong Kong after she got divorced, Lucy hadn't seen her for some time. She believed she was dead—that was until last month, when she ran into her on Peel Street.

They came across each other by chance, each as awfully attired as the other, gawking at each other in disbelief, believing that the other was an apparition, their memories of sisterhood long forgotten amid their separate existences.

It was only after Lucy muttered, 'Jessica?' that they instantly hurled themselves on top of each other, Lucy holding on tight ready for love, while Jessica wailed, scratching her. Lucy tried to hold her down, but Jessica was furious like a wild cat, targeting her face and arms. Lucy only retaliated, wanting to free herself from the vicious shouts and curses.

Then suddenly, a strange hairy man—Monkey- wearing a tight gray suit had separated them, shouting, 'Stop! Buddha says it's better to conquer yourself than fight a thousand battles.'

Lucy had tried to smile at her sister, but Jessica's mouth was open, saliva hanging from her vengeful face. She looked upon Lucy in disgust and spat at her, then the police came and took them away separately. They hadn't seen each other since, too old and stubborn now to go back and salvage what they had. The story quickly circulated throughout the island about the twins, and several rumors along with it.

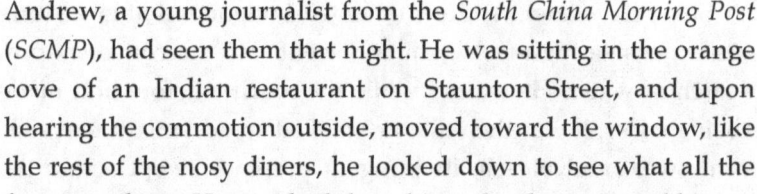

Andrew, a young journalist from the *South China Morning Post* (*SCMP*), had seen them that night. He was sitting in the orange cove of an Indian restaurant on Staunton Street, and upon hearing the commotion outside, moved toward the window, like the rest of the nosy diners, he looked down to see what all the fuss was about. He watched them hit each other, cry, and hiss.

He overheard a pretty Indian girl beside him say, 'That's them, that's the twins, the ones with the wealthy husband.'

THE COFFEE SHOP MASQUERADE

He walked into the office the next day and mentioned it to his editor, who was in the throes of coming down from the recent successful sales of the Lee family murder trial and was interested in picking up more Hong Kong family dynasty stories—stories filled with money and intrigue—and so with her permission, Andrew was able to investigate the real story behind the twins.

Unsurprisingly, the police were accommodating. It helped when he passed over a couple of $100 bills. Armed with their full names, he had searched through the *SCMP* archives and was surprised when he saw their photos emerge on the screen: two beautiful young women at a debutante ball. There they were, smiling with delight in their new position. There were also photos of their father, including one in which he was holding a large cigar deep in laughter with Nöel Coward. Digging further, he had learned about the father's successes—the buildings, the money, a widower pictured with many women, but devoted to his two daughters: Lucy, a girl with her eye on running the business, and Jessica, an athletic girl devoted to charity work. There wasn't much in the archives after the father sold the buildings, not until his death. Lucy was named as his successor, but her sister seemed to disappear from the papers like a good story gone sour. Andrew didn't read much into this, he thought he would just do a profile to end the rumors about a Chinese husband.

Some days later, Andrew emerged invigorated after visiting his expensive high-tech gym and went into the coffee shop in search of water. He waited while the tourists before him made their choices. It was then that he smelled an odd mixture of stale cold sweat and bleach, its pungent presence swept across the room. Thinking it was him, he looked down, embarrassed, but as the tourists in front turned and looked past him, they whispered. He followed their eyes, and saw Lucy standing right behind him, her nose twitched as she mouthed the menu. He didn't know what to do and stood still, he realized that this was his chance to talk to her. He didn't know what to say, but being a good reporter, he knew that he couldn't let her get away and saw that her aggravation was escalating over being the center of stares, he turned and asked her, 'Confusing, isn't it?'

'What?'

'I said it's confusing, trying to figure out what is what. I mean, how many coffees can there be? Americano?' He then moved toward her as she kept staring up at the board. 'Macchiato? It just doesn't make sense. Why do they have to complicate it all? All I want is a black coffee. No sugar, just a normal black coffee.'

One of the ladies in front looked back at him, she believed that he was talking to her. 'Oh, I know, why can't they just tell you what's what?'

He smiled back, not wanting this to become a group discussion, but Lucy had peered at him in shock, then up again at the board.

'I don't understand the ice,' she said, alarmed that she was hearing her own voice talking. 'What's an iced latte?'

'I'm not sure,' he said, pretending he didn't know. 'I know, why don't I buy you one?'

She laughed out loud at him. 'Buy me one?' She then grabbed his arm tight, letting the laughter flow through her body. 'You want to buy me a coffee, one of those iced things?'

'Sure,' he said, smiling at her. He grew aware that all eyes were upon them, but he didn't care. There could be something here, something that could put him over the top and make it front page material.

'Okay,' she said, embarrassed, but pleased.

'Great, why don't you sit down over there?' He pointed to the red couch that had suddenly become empty.

THE COFFEE SHOP MASQUERADE

She looked at him suspiciously. It had been a long time since she had sat down with anyone, she hardly knew what to do and immediately believed his intentions were not honorable. She thought she would be better off warning him now.

'No funny business, okay?' she said, shaking her index finger.

He laughed nervously and stared at her old dirty fingernail. 'No, no funny business.'

She sat down and looked around apprehensively. She felt nervous, as if all eyes were on her. She looked down at the front cover of a magazine, with a picture of a strange woman carrying a pear.

'Stupid cover,' she said, unaware that she said it out loud. She realized this and looked around and was relieved to see that no one had noticed her, not even that annoying boy behind the counter. She turned her attention to the people. It appeared as if everyone was just moving along like they were on an invisible conveyer belt, sipping on their coffees as they went out.

Nervously she patted down her hair and fixed her rotted cardigan. She started to play with the ragged skin on her inner palm that had become dislodged after one of the nights bleaching the walls. She had done that thinking that the walls were running with slime, deadly bacteria that circulated throughout the building. Strange images like this often invaded her mind. When she was young, she used to see men or monsters lurking behind trees. When she would turn to look back at them, they would quickly hide or disappear, but she had always felt that they were always there watching. She had once tried to explain it to her father, but he only hushed her, telling her that an imagination that size wouldn't get her anywhere. Then the bacteria, which came right after her father died, millions of amoebas falling down the walls like a turbulent waterfall heavy in its velocity. They then dispersed, rushing to infect her and her surroundings. In a panic, she had splashed bleach across the walls straight from the bottle. The smell had been overpowering, but Lucy was afraid that if she opened the windows, more bacteria would infiltrate the room. She decided to sleep on the bathroom floor, allowing the fumes to destroy her lungs.

She looked over at the young man; he was busy saying something to the boy. She couldn't understand what it was, then an alarming thought came into her head that he was going to poison her. He and the boy were in it together — they planned to kill her — but she stopped that destructive thought when he came toward her carrying a tray with 10 small espresso cups.

'I thought,' he said confidently as he sat down beside her, 'that we should have a coffee tasting. Then we can both be clear about what's what.'

Lucy didn't know what to say, and she sat dumbfounded at this gesture. She watched him swivel the miniature cups around, as he squinted trying to read the messy black writing.

'So here, this is ... an Americano. Oh,' he said, looking at the tray, 'we need sugar.' Andrew jumped up like a rabbit to grab sachets.

Lucy, found this all strange, but her curiosity for actually tasting these new coffee concoctions overwhelmed her, and she started to taste the Americano.

Andrew came back, smiling. 'So, how is it?'

'It's like a normal black coffee.'

He tried it, 'You're right!' He looked down at the other cups that waited their turn. He picked up the one closest to him and passed it to her. 'This one's a latte.'

She tried it. It was milky, soft, and not strong; she went in for a second taste.

'Why are you doing this?' she spoke suddenly, her mind so used to being the sole listener of its thoughts.

'What do you mean? I want to try the coffee.'

'No,' she continued, 'with me. Why are you sitting with me?'

'Why? What's wrong with you?'

'People, they think I'm mad, crazy.' she hissed the words like a snake.

Andrew sat back and stared at her. 'Are you crazy?'

'No, I don't think so, I think,' she then started to point with her finger at people in the coffee shop and squinted her eyes, 'I think they're crazy.'

'Do you think I'm crazy?' he asked her.

She looked down at his clothes; he looked like he had come out of church with his white tunic top and his brown sandals. His hair was thick, and he grew it long enough to be able to push it back from his face. Sometimes he wore a very delicate leather headband that kept it in place, but he decided wisely not to wear it today. He appeared religious, but safe.

'You,' she said, laughing. 'No, you're okay. You good-looking boy.'

It was odd, he thought, but when she spoke, he could hear a trace of a local accent, singing and short. He smiled at her compliment, being used to hearing it often before. He didn't mind the fact that he was good looking, as it did make life easier in some ways, but at work, he was the pretty boy, so it was decided he thought, that he should work on the society pages. Being a relatively new arrival, he was still new to the whole game here. But he became good at ignoring stares from lustful local boys at the office, but it was hard meeting someone here, a girl that he could really talk to. He had thoughts about his editor, but she seemed so frazzled and on edge that he sensibly stayed away, leaving those thoughts about her in the safe vicinity of his mind.

'Have you lived in Hong Kong long?'

'Yes, many, many years,' she nodded, as she slurped the next coffee. It was sour, and she started to scratch away the top lining of her tongue with her teeth. She glanced down at the black writing, which read 'Sumatra.'

'Ugh,' she shuddered, looking up at him with childish eyes, 'I bet you can't guess how long I've lived here.'

He shook his head.

'Many years, long before you were born.'

He smiled, knowing full well that she had lived here since she was five, her mother died at childbirth, and her father never remarried.

He decided to play it safe and ask the question that everyone asks when she interrupted him: 'How old you think I am?'

He hardly knew what to say, 'Umm, I'm not sure.'

'Yes, come on, take a guess.' She waved her hand at him, holding her small, stained cloth bag closer to herself for protection in case he guessed wrong and destroyed her illusion. She didn't like to look in the mirror, as she often didn't know the woman staring back. Sometimes she was playful, sometimes sad, sometimes just numb, but she now regretted not looking at herself today and wished she was wearing some sort of makeup. She must still have some lying around.

'Okay,' he considered, he thought it was probably best to cut it down seven years from her real age, so he said, 'Fifty-five?'

'No!' she said triumphantly, beating her hand down on the table. The coffee cups jumped but only spat out single droplets. 'I'm 59,' she said proudly.

'Really?' he said, dabbing at the spill with thin napkins.

'Yes,' she replied, nodding profusely, overjoyed by his mistake, and oblivious to the mess she just made.

He smiled, thinking that the myth about women lying about their age was true. To be honest, she looked 65, but now he felt he had secured her confidence.

'Shall we try some more?' He motioned to the cups.

'Yes,' she said, bending in toward him, 'why not?'

They tried a couple more, a selection of different coffees from Africa and Brazil. Some were bitter and harsh, like the angry wind that hits you when you're walking along the beach, while others were delicate and tasteless, like the pale gelatin coating of dim sums. She didn't like the dryness of Peruvian coffee, but enjoyed the hint of jam from Ethiopian beans, while he favored the contrasting sweetness from Honduras. They spent the morning tasting all the coffees the barista could offer. He came over to them, gently bending over to explain the coffee varieties and where they came from. He spoke clearly and concisely, like good sommeliers at five-star hotels, with the same grace and respect for coffee that sommeliers had for wine. They sat there appreciating his effort.

'What do you do here?' she asked him.

'I work for a newspaper.'

She nodded like she already knew.

He continued. '*The South China Morning Post.*' He saw her begin to change with the caffeine inside of her. She started to play with the swirls of baby hair from her upper neck; she was trying to flirt with him. He politely smiled, alert to the ways of women, experienced with enough flirt-filled gestures to recognize that this was one. He liked how she was trying. Her legs started swaying, and he watched her upper body try and copy them.

'Are you a reporter?' she asked.

He noticed that her accent was returning to its native state, her local role was diminishing.

'Yes, I am.'

'Do you know who I am?'

He looked at her, unsure of what to say, but he decided it was better to lie. 'No, I don't.'

She smiled to herself and crossed her arms.

'Should I know?'

She shook her head, 'No, I'm no one special.'

He had no idea where this was going. 'How long have you lived here?'

'Most of my life,' she said, her eyes focused on the enormous piece of chocolate cake being paraded through the coffee shop. Its owner ordered a dollop of cream to accompany it, and she admired how the boy carried it over proudly. The owner took it from him greedily and continued with his conversation, forgetting to thank the boy.

'That's rude,' Lucy said suddenly.

'What is?'

'That man, he didn't even say 'thank you. How rude!' she spoke loudly.

A couple beside them looked over, meeting Lucy's eyes as she said, 'That man didn't say 'thank you.'' She pointed at the man deep in his gluttonous state.

The couple looked at each other and chose to ignore her.

'Isn't that awful?' she continued loudly, unaware of the scene she was creating. Andrew stared at her, helplessly trying to calm her down, but she started banging her hands down again, rocking the table, and without warning, she got up.

'Well, that's it—how dare he!' she said. With wild eyes, she looked into those of Andrew, who was trying to sink deeper into the red couch. He was about to stop her, say something, but he couldn't, and he just sat and watched her walk over to the man.

'Excuse me,' she said.

The man looked up, surprised, and immediately held his head back from the sour smell that she also brought with her. 'You didn't say 'thank you.''

'What? Are you taking the piss?' He spoke with an Australian drawl, and his bouffant of graying hair amassed upon his head didn't move, as if it was trapped under his skinny black sunglasses.

'You didn't say 'thank you' to the boy you brought you this.'

'So?' he replied with a smirk.

'So?' Lucy mimicked him, she allowed her emotional memories to surface. She could almost feel her father speaking from within her. 'That's typical, you, you Australian mongrel, you wouldn't know manners if they slapped you in the face. You're a disgrace to civilization, you and your germs.'

This caused both men to start laughing hysterically.

'No, love, I think you're the one with the germs.'

'What?' She shook her head, suddenly shocked.

'You're the problem with the germs, love,' he said, pinching his nose, 'and the smell, don't you wash?'

Lucy stood, traumatized. 'You, you can see germs on me?'

'Yes, love, they're practically jumping all over you.'

Lucy, in a panic, rushed out of the coffee shop, she screamed as she went, desperate to wash these infectious things off her.

Andrew stood there defeated. He could feel eyes looking at him, but he didn't care. The two Australian men kept on laughing, clapping their hands together in celebration of their victory.

'Andrew?'

He heard his name, but he couldn't bear to see who it was. He hoped it wasn't one of those girls who had accosted him yesterday on the stairs. 'You look like a Hot Jesus' one of them had said. He turned around. Thankfully, it wasn't. It was Grace, one of his football friends' wives.

He smiled at her, confused.

'Are you okay?' She asked, placing her left hand on his elbow.

He nodded, 'Yeah, just a strange lady.'

———∽∽———

When Andrew returned to work that afternoon, his editor didn't mention anything about the twin story at their weekly meeting. Apparently, most of the major banks' chairmen were now making plans to move back to live in Hong Kong, in an attempt to enable them to receive their annual bonuses in peace. His editor was too busy trying to figure out how this would affect Hong Kong society.

The following week, Andrew read a small piece in *The South China Morning Post* about an unnamed local woman in intensive care suffering from severe bleach burns. He just scanned it and moved on, not realizing it was Lucy.

5

THE RED COUCH

Good travelers leave no tracks.
–Tao Te Ching

The red couch in the coffee shop had been constructed on the mainland in a small furniture factory owned by a father and son. They'd worked hard to keep and maintain orders over the years, but as soon as the father became ill, then died, the factory ran at a loss and cut corners. The red couch was one of the last pieces constructed there, and the piece of red faux leather was stapled on roughly to the frame by the son himself. He'd cried as he made it, remembering all the good times he'd had with his father. His tears stained the wood underneath. He recalled what his father often said: *There are no guarantees in life, nothing except death and taxes.*

The mask in the storeroom heard the red couch creak. It was soaked in emotions from the conversations that it replayed softly — desperate to hear them it called out to the couch, but it didn't reply.

The spirit in the mask didn't like where it was. Like so much of its life before Mario and Nonna, it was hidden away. Sometimes it caused storeroom doors to open and close, it picked up and moved coffee cups to strange locations, creating movement in the shop that was already filled with vibrations left over from the day.

Monkey sat on the roof across from the coffee shop. He liked Soho with its bars and people. He could hide easily when he needed to. Sometimes he could hear a voice calling, but it was ever so slight, like the wind when it was sad. It whispered sorrowful woes. He thought it must be the mask. Mario must have left it around here, but he had yet to find it. Monkey wasn't allowed to enter any shops — that was part of the agreement between those in power and himself. Don't bring unnecessary attention to yourself, he was told. Too many rules, he thought, even from Buddha — don't do this, Monkey; be good, Monkey; listen to your people, Monkey. Don't poke fun at the Jade Emperor.

The coffee shop was closed now. The cleaner had arrived promptly, fresh from temple, the smell of incense lingered in her hair. She had prayed for her daughter to get away from her husband, a bad brute. How she wished they had more money, more power.

She didn't have to stay long, just a light dusting, reorganize the chairs, and wipe down the tables with a thick damp cloth. She failed to remove the stains that lay embedded deep within the scratches and the small dents that surrounded the circular tables, like small bites from a child.

There was no treasure for her today as she finished feeling down into the red couch. Occasionally, she would find small coins — or a ring and one time, a $100 note — but nothing today.

Her back hurt as she straightened herself, then she glanced over toward the chaotic wooden magazine rack and headed over to it. Old magazines that had fallen down the side of the red couch were forgotten. She restored order to the rack, but she was unable to read very well, so the magazines were arranged on the rack randomly.

THE COFFEE SHOP MASQUERADE

Finished for the day, she pushed the alarm button, its siren forcing her to maneuver quickly around the neatly aligned furniture to reach the door, which closed with a sharp click, leaving the alarm to sound into the emptiness. It warned all those small parasites in the vicinity to remain docile. The screeching stopped suddenly, allowing the last beat to vibrate into the stillness of the shop, its lights were off, its chairs unoccupied, and the coffee machine's small red buttons now dormant—no sound, no steam, no power. They rested.

The walls remained free from the sudden temperature shifts, with no vapor stimulating their paintwork, and no spills trying to permeate the glossy floor. The room was quiet, free from the usual sounds of dripping, falling sugar crystals, and the whirring of pale thin stirrers. The cheap chairs no longer groaned from bearing various weights of customers, and the tables were no longer poor substitutes for desks, encumbered with small laptops. The room, like the air, held its breath, as it waited for life to arrive and fill it with meaning.

A small neon sign shaped like a red coffee cup outside reminded others of the role it played during the day. Taxi headlights shone their way through the window, but their beams didn't reach the counter, the pristine silver machines that patiently awaited action, the plastic and ceramic cups lined up ready for service, or the stains on the wooden floors from clumsy hands.

The coffee shop sat halfway up the hill, well-protected from the bitterness of sea swells. The modern skyscrapers below barricaded it in. It was easier to look down then up due to the chaotic balance of buildings and signs on the hill. To pale eyes, it was strenuous to look up. They were more suited to looking down. No sea air floated through the cavities of the side streets, looking to cool and spray its spit upon wanderers, as shielded walls of concrete and steel banished it.

The road it sat on was one of constant change from newly themed restaurants that invented fresh ploys to attract crowds, to the continuous line of red taxis that drove through it, yet everything remained the same. Similar conversations leapt throughout the road, bouncing with loud drunk laughter in an attempt to be a home away from home.

The spirit in the mask stirred again as a gentle whiff of incense reached the lost and found box in the storeroom, a familiar smell that caused the door to open and shut. It recalled an old song—no words, just soft notes—bells, cymbals, flutes—they'd all meant something once. It felt itself rise from the mask and entered the shop.

It saw the red couch resting in the right-hand corner, elevated and accessible via two wooden steps. A tall, dusty fern stood beside the shallow steps like a grand marble foo dog at the entrance to a great house. Its leaves were dusty, making it appear false and forgotten, but it was alive, absorbing the cold air that had stopped it from yellowing, its chlorophyll frozen within the air conditioning.

The spirit wandered through the shop. A blackboard with small writing—*a thought for the day*—hung above the coffee collection counter, though the 'thought' hadn't been changed in a few weeks, currently quoting Kierkegaard: *Be that self which one truly is.*

Small stands surrounded the counter, each filled with the company's own coffee beans in black, shiny bags with labels depicting exotic, dated images of Hawaii, Colombia, and Jamaica. Their presence cramped the counter, making it more difficult to see further into the glass cabinet that held hard icy cakes. Small pieces of cake sat in there now—one piece of chocolate cake, half a carrot cake that was too sweet, and a banana loaf that had been in there for over a week, its corners now turning green.

Ceramic mugs stood patiently, their open faces down. Displaying the company's small trademark, they faced the clean, empty coffeepot that would fill them in the morning. A stack of freshly washed plates accompanied the cups. The first plate still had a stain on it that the old dishwasher was unable to remove.

The alarm's green activation light sat snug in a corner, its warning light on. Everything was imprisoned, leaving the shop compressed and tense.

The aroma of coffee no longer floated through the shop. Beans were now safely within jars, bags, and the freezer in the tiny storeroom.

Honking sounds filtered in from outside. A woman looking the wrong way nearly got killed by a speeding taxi. She was deathly silent after her mistake, while the taxi driver shouted out to her.

No moonlight shone through the clouds as they covered the sky like a child's thick dark painting—only artificial yellow and blue tinted lights lined the roads. The mechanical stairs beside the shop made their last run, their movement seizing from rubbing the sides of the shop. Everything was settled and waiting.

Throughout the small hours, voices reverberated in silence all that was said the day before— the insincere greetings, surprise encounters, and uncomfortable stares from strangers. These thoughts and emotions were absorbed in its brick walls, relaying silent voices throughout its night vigil. Invisible Wi-Fi waves hovered throughout the shop, their vibrations the only life as they darted through the darkness like thin webs from weak spiders that hid in the corners. It was hard for life to survive in this shop filled with the unnatural.

The spirit gently circulated, then rested on the red couch, absorbing all the thoughts of those who'd sat here, smiling at the silliness and odd language, but after a while, it felt sad. Everything was the same—after thousands of years, the thoughts were identical: People still worried about love, money, family—so much for the mind's evolution.

It looked out into the night and watched a group of people pass. A woman made a comment about the coffee shop. One of the men heard her and stopped to examine it. She walked forward away from him, leaving the glass to capture his eyes as they followed her. It reflected a look filled with anxiety, hope, and love.

A wandering old man hobbled past—unable to sleep for more than four hours a night, as his back ached after years of working at the port. He stared into the coffee shop toward the red couch. The spirit felt his eyes. As he scanned the shop, he saw a lone coffee cup standing on the counter—had it been forgotten? He wondered whether it was supposed to be there, filled with some sort of cleaning solution or perhaps it was a token reminder about something. He looked through the refection at his own aging eyes, remembering how he used to leave strange articles out like that to remind him to do mundane things. He left the window unaware that his fingers had smudged the glass and shuffled away toward the noise of banging shutters

The red couch started to hush. The spirit saw that it was home to pieces that had floated off a thousand bodies. Skin fragments, body hair, dust from home. The sweat from foreign bodies had seeped through the red couch, its stench hidden behind the exterior, unable to be eradicated by mere cloths—a repulsive reminder of the many who passed through—pieces of customers forever laid to rest in the shop. Tourists' vocal orders saturated the walls, leaving the shop filled with whispers of past conversations as impatient sighs and anxious moods relived their role. Grime and grit from foreign soles of other worlds far away lay underneath the freshly washed floors.

Voices from outside penetrated the shop, their noises sounding muffled and loud. A girl rushed past the dark windows afraid to see her drunken crying face in its reflection.

Along the road, small restaurants were starting to close as the full crowd started to move south toward the rickety stairs, taking their money and thirst with them. On their way down, they walked along a busy road filled with arrogant galleries showcasing items from another reality of life lived only by the few.

The taxis stopped driving past the coffee shop, leaving the crooked tarmac alone. Most diners had gone home by now.

The city lay in slumber. Small snorts exhaled from its trees as the mountain moans of its sore sides littered with heavy constructions built without its consent. Wire cables throbbed into the night, massaging the mound's aching shoulders.

Monkey got down from the roof and walked around the surrounding streets. He was wearing dirty tracksuit pants and an XL T-shirt that read *Welcome to Hell*. He liked this area at night because it was quiet, and he was free to stand and stare into the various shops. He was fascinated with how many strange things man had created for himself — silly things that served no purpose, but that man would gladly pay a lot of money to have.

He walked past the coffee shop and looked inside. The spirit saw him and hid. It was an old instinct. The spirit recognized its old owner, and for a moment considered showing itself, but didn't. Monkey could wait another day. The spirit recalled their first meeting, the old witch on the island had offered Monkey a book as payment after Monkey had rescued her sow from the water demon.

Monkey had turned his nose up and asked, 'Why would I want that witch? I know everything! Give me some money.'

The witch shook her head, 'I don't have use for money.'

Monkey then saw the mask in the corner, it was painted golden then and shone beautifully. 'What about that mask? Can I have that?'

She had replied, 'No, she is too powerful Monkey, too powerful for you.'

Monkey huffed he didn't like being told no and so when her back was turned Monkey snatched the mask and left quickly on a cloud. He had mumbled, 'Witches never have any money, what is the point of being a witch when you can't use spells for money. Old hags.' He placed the mask in a cave that he thought no one would find. A small treasure trove where he kept things. Unfortunately, a century ago some curious white people did, finders' keepers some would say.

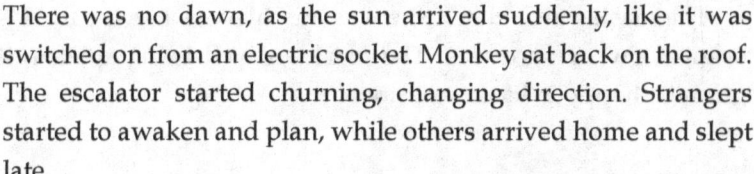

There was no dawn, as the sun arrived suddenly, like it was switched on from an electric socket. Monkey sat back on the roof. The escalator started churning, changing direction. Strangers started to awaken and plan, while others arrived home and slept late.

The spirit sensed the dawn and returned to the box, maneuvering itself and showing its face. It wanted to be out in the open again, how it missed Nonna's conversations.

Soon, a girl arrived, her hair a mess. She unlocked the door, and the shop exhaled. She rushed in, switching off the screeches that warned of a disturbance and left the door slightly ajar in hopes of bringing in the morning. She opened the storeroom door and saw the mask staring at her. She grinned — a joke? Maybe something to annoy Patrick, the manager?

She picked up the mask and spoke to it. 'Hello there. Now where shall I place you? Somewhere where you can see

THE COFFEE SHOP MASQUERADE

everything — somewhere that will annoy Patrick.'

Monkey stirred — the mask had moved. It was close, but where? Somewhere around here, halfway up a hill, Monkey thought, but there was no satisfaction halfway up, no goal completed, only a mere transit place for the weary traveler.

The girl in the shop placed the mask on the open shelf behind the counter, beside the dusty board and fake plants.

'There.' she said to the mask, 'you can see everything now. Now how else can we annoy Patrick? I know! Let's decorate the whole shop.'

The girl entered the storeroom and grabbed the tired looking boxes labelled 'CNY festive decorations' for Chinese New Year.

She carried one out and said, 'What do you think, mask? Shall we start with the dragon?'

She took out an old paper dragon and placed it on the shelf beside the mask. 'Oh yes, Patrick will love that!' she laughed.

The mask watched her; she was mischievous like the mask's original owner once was. The mask enjoyed being spoken. It grinned, happy in its new position.

6

New Year's Wishes

Bad fortune rests upon good fortune.
Good luck hides within bad luck.
  –Tao Te Ching

Patrick was the coffee shop's lead barista and manager. He was proud of his position and took his job very seriously. He was on his way to work taking the bus early from his home in Tung Chung. His eyes were closed. A slight roar from a stranger's phone irritated him as it replayed vulgar cartoons. The surprise of the first bell aroused Patrick's eyes, and he stared drowsily out the tinted window down to the highway. He watched five workers lazily stumble off the tangerine bus and make their way to the newly built MTR station. Patrick felt the bus's axle lift as it started to drive toward the Tsing Ma Bridge. The morning's thick smog encased the bus as it sped around the corner of the chipped mountain layered in grand Chinese graves. Suddenly, the silver metropolis of the city center stood tall thinly covered in a transparent layer of toxic yellow fog blown over from Shenzhen.

The bell sounded again. Patrick rose slowly, accidentally touching the knee of the sleepy man beside him. Standing in line waiting his turn to leave the bus, he yawned loudly, his hands hitting the woman behind him.

THE COFFEE SHOP MASQUERADE

Sifting his way through the maze of dark-haired strangers, with the occasional burst of blond, he noticed that most of their eyes were staring at the floor as they balanced their heavy overpacked rucksacks or slim line designer briefcases.

Patrick breathed in the early morning energy and felt invigorated. He relished the morning rush hour. Here, he thought, is where I belong—among these important producers of worldwide economic commerce, a phrase he picked up from a copy of *The Economist* magazine that was left on a table in the coffee shop. He was part of this city, serving these masses, making their mornings a little bit gentler by supplying them with a service.

He walked fast, allowing himself to be carried away by the importance of the grand concrete surroundings, with their over-designed fountains and uncomfortable constructed benches.

It was early Monday morning. The city was still tired and yawned from its hectic weekend. Most commuters left Patrick's side once they hit Central, but he continued straight up the hill. The escalator ran against him, helping those from the mountain come down efficiently.

Patrick enjoyed walking up the stairs, he jumped enthusatically like a hyper child two steps at a time. He passed a bald man carrying two gigantic teddy bears. Feeling their soft fur brush against his hand, he looked back at the bored-looking man, wondering why he was carrying two toys this size. His thoughts nearly caused him to walk into a small local woman rushing to work. He apologized and started to contemplate the week ahead. Being a Monday meant that he had to organize the forthcoming week's events; from setting up the promotional stands to soft launching a new jasmine green tea matcha latte.

Although he was the lead barista, Patrick didn't understand the word. He had nodded when they told him the title, trying to appear relaxed, he pretended to know what it meant. '*Barista*,' he practiced. Still, he couldn't pronounce it correctly, he said the first part fast and ending it on a high note with the 'ta,' Bars-tttaaaa. But now he was beginning to train the two girls. He hoped that they would soon come to grips with the job's importance so that he could deal with more important managerial tasks, such as the budget and planning more exciting events for the Chinese New Year charity effort.

A collection was taken in the shop throughout the year in a small Pyrex box that sat beside the till, labeled with the name of a children's hospital that needed funds. Patrick's coffee shop had fallen short on profits last year, and he was embarrassed by his boss into doing something about it, but he had yet to think what could give him the edge over the rest, as the dated marketing ploys the company had suggested failed to bring in anything.

He recently thought about starting a coffee-tasting evening after that man asked him to make samples of each of the coffees on the menu. He had taken the request seriously, fulfilling the quota. It did bother him though, as he assumed most people knew what each coffee tasted like. Clearly, they didn't, and he pondered how to use that. He remembered some manual that the company had thrown at him about finding a niche, that hole in the market, try something a bit different. Perhaps he thought, the company could find some coffee expert for him — but why not him? He could learn what was best to drink in the morning and in the evening, he could describe the different varieties of coffee. He visualized himself explaining carefully what was what to a large audience of appreciative people. They would listen and be impressed by his knowledge, then the company might hear about it, and he might get promoted further to take over the flagship shop in Pacific Place or IFC, but this was a long way off, he thought, just as he saw an old man wheel out festive

THE COFFEE SHOP MASQUERADE

decoration.

His week was busy planning for Chinese New Year. It was quickly approaching, and Patrick already noticed the trickle of red packets and happy Buddhas stuck to the normally bland windows of Fortress. It was only a matter of time before they exploded and were seen everywhere. Last Saturday, he had taken out the tired looking boxes labelled 'CNY festive decorations' and placed them in the middle of the storeroom. He had written on a slip of receipt paper, *please not move*, instructing the Sunday staff to leave them for him. He wrote it in English, a method he sometimes used to try and stress its importance.

Confident in this approach, he opened the back door to the dark coffee shop and punched in an 11-number pin to deactivate the vicious-sounding alarm. He immediately noticed the lone cup on the counter, walked over to it, and cautiously peered into it. There was nothing, so he placed the cup on top of the heap ready for consumption. Patrick failed to notice that the bathroom door was open.

Returning to the back, he opened the back door wide. Looking up at the thick cloudy sky, he stood still and listened, as he could hear musical cymbals clashing, then Chinese music playing. They must be starting practice for upcoming events, though it's a bit early, he thought. He couldn't see that it was just Monkey on the opposite roof banging cymbals he had found on the back of a truck. Monkey was singing and smiling as he banged. 'Come out, come out wherever you are, mask!'

Back in the coffee shop Patrick turned on the lights, and his eyes immediately were drawn to the festive decoration boxes, which sat ravaged in the middle of the floor. Most of the festive contents were oddly placed around the coffee shop. He saw the red lanterns hanging from thin invisible threads and a group of giggling monks sitting in the corner beside the plastic fern.

Disturbed at the lack of order, he was unaware that the Sunday staff had messily placed things around just to annoy him. Oblivious, he didn't realize that they often laughed at his strict silly ways and the odd notes he left for them in English.

Those lazy pigs, typical Sunday staff. I bet they haven't even replenished the sticks and the sweetener table. He swore gently as he gathered up the Chinese caricatures of Buddha and the golden coins that sat happily on the red couch. He turned and looked at the counter and saw the mask and dragon facing him. He wondered whether that was the same mask from the storeroom. It appeared less scary out here. He walked toward it. It looked good there, almost as if it was grinning. He took down the dragon but left the mask.

Placing the items on the counter, he looked out at the glistening road. The morning's murky sun now bounced off the mirrored windows of the majestic buildings and glared a single stream of light onto the freshly washed road. Patrick sighed heavily and returned to the staff room. Hanging up his thin gray jacket, he grabbed one of the newly washed aprons lying on the chair, tore off its soft plastic cover, and shook it out to revive it after its journey to the cleaners.

He took two latex gloves from the box on the shelf, he put them on carefully and grabbed the expensive double-sided tape he had purchased last week to help him place the fabricated posters on the front window with the utmost care. Returning to the counter, he stared at the posters, mentally devising where each one should be placed. The red lanterns were fine, but the disaster of last year's sloppy display remained fresh in his mind. He had left it up to the girls, but they were too distracted, discussing the new mall opening, and they had made a shambles of it. There was no structure to it, no story considered. They rolled their eyes when he tried to reason with them, trying to explain the importance, but they didn't care. Those two had left. Thankfully, he didn't have to fire them, as one got married and the other went to work for a firm in Quarry Bay.

He grabbed hold of Buddha and he took him to the window. Taking care he held his breath, he didn't want to leave fingerprint smudges or careless breath marks that would stick to the seamless clear glass. On the outside glass, he could see the markings of some strangers' fingerprints, but he would attend to those later.

He opened the main door and walked outside into the daylight. He stood there and scrutinized his work—Buddha's gluttonous happy face, his bald head gleaming as his hands were filled with solid gold coins. Patrick's hands, encased in ghostly latex gloves, hung down at his sides, his fingers slightly curved as he examined the thick paper closely. He heard some girls giggling and an old woman shouting something, but he closed his eyes, held his breath, and counted internally. He knew from the previous year that if the poster was going to fall, it would happen in the first few moments of its inhabitation on the glass—or more likely, it would fall alone in the middle of the night away from the disruption of the crowd. His mind turned toward the other coffee shops, especially that small dirty place in Central: What characters would they place in their windows to show their customers that they also knew of the importance of the time? He already had read their Chinese New Year specials online—all little attempts to win their customers' affections and spread their own good luck. Patrick sulked. Why couldn't his company's marketing department be more generous with its budget? He looked around at all the celebratory articles he had. He wasn't blessed with designer pictures—photos with slick, modern approaches on what Chinese New Year meant.

Using his own initiative and creativity, and thanks to the tight-fisted corporation he worked for, he had to use stale, two-year-old decorations. How he yearned for the lead suspension cables that were drilled into the ceiling, able to accommodate new seasonal displays, which would allow for a simple change of posters from Christmas to Chinese New Year in seconds. Patrick sighed softly after his minutes of monitoring the posters ended, he sensed a taxicab slowing down the driver had lowered the windows. Patrick hopped back inside.

He removed the latex gloves, and looked up at the clock — 6 a.m. he placed his café-latte-colored name tag on his crisp red apron, and moved behind the counter, he started to warm up the machines and switched on the lights. He went over and locked the front door, as he didn't want to risk any unwelcome early customers.

He heard a delivery truck driving toward him and listened as the sprinkling of workers sweeping up the remains of the latest rowdy Sunday night. He placed himself behind the coffee workstation, and started to bang on the filters, releasing their almost cemented debris. The Sunday staff hadn't cleaned the machine properly. Patrick stood listening as the machines started to stir, awakening like a hissing steam train, with their relays pushing and pulling. He looked up at the mask, which seemed to be staring at him.

Patrick smiled at it. 'Good morning, mask.' he said softly. He remembered that when he asked Ruth about it, she said some white guy found it by the red couch. Why would someone leave a mask?

Suddenly, Coco and Jasmine banged on the window, they were giggling .

He looked up, irritated. 'You're late!' he barked in their native tongue. He walked over and unlatched the lock, and they giggled further.

'Yeah, what are you going to do?' Coco retaliated. She looked at the grinning Jasmine and rolled her eyes, and they walked into the back, where they took off their layers. They were still giggling loudly when the first customer of the day walked in. Patrick opened the storeroom door and quieted them. He turned around and greeted an overweight Australian man who already was deep into his second hour of sweating. His light cotton lemon shirt highlighted the dribbles of sweat that fell off his back. He smirked confidently at Patrick and raised his eyes to stare at the menu.

He tapped his fat, wet fingers on the brown counter as he uttered 'Ummm…'

'Yes, sir?' Patrick said quickly. He had seen this man before. He had ordered that enormous piece of cake with cream that the crazy lady had shouted at him about. Patrick considered that maybe she was concerned with the size of him and tried to tell him not to eat so much, leading him to think that she wasn't that crazy, only lonely, a thought that evoked something in him, for he knew loneliness well. He realigned his thoughts, attempting not to stare at the sweat beads that had formed on the Australian's forehead that were now beginning to change direction and head south. Patrick bit down on his lower lip, in an attempt to control his urge to gag. His judgment took possession, he thought, how could this man be this sweaty already? It was only 53 degrees Fahrenheit this morning. How could he let himself become this size? Doesn't he have a wife?

Suddenly, the door opened, another stranger walked in, and Patrick remembered himself.

'Yeah,' the Australian man said, 'I guess I'll take a large double iced cafe latte.'

'Yes, sir!' Patrick replied jovially as he looked over at the ice machine. His eyes grew large when he realized it was empty.

'Umm, one moment, sir, I just have to get ice,' Patrick spoke in a strong, very broken Cantonese accent. He had taken the standard English classes at school, but never excelled or felt the need to take more. Kind, polite foreigners had informed him that he spoke very good English, and after that confirmation, he no longer felt the need to improve. He smiled at the confused Australian and ran into the storeroom.

He walked in on Coco and Jasmine comparing their expensive new Hello Kitty purses, he interrupted them harshly. 'Where's the ice?'

'I don't know, mama's boy, why don't you check the freezer?' Jasmine said. Coco quickly fell into hysterics, this caused Patrick to become red-faced.

His mother had visited him at work every week since he had started, but after winning some money in Macau, she had started coming in more often, she ordered strong coffee that she hated and bossed him around in front of his staff. It wasn't very professional. He had tried to explain this to her, but she didn't care. It only fueled her desire to visit more often and embarrass him further.

Patrick grunted and shook his head, he muttered, 'Why is it always me?'

He located the ice while quietly cursing Coco and Jasmine and returned to the front counter triumphantly holding a black plastic bucket filled with ice. Coco and Jasmine followed and jumped into work. They busily served the three other customers of the early morning while the oversized, perspiring Australian stood at the side staring into space. Patrick looked at him and lifted the bucket. 'See, sir,' he pointed to the bucket of ice, 'one moment, Sir.'

The Australian motioned with a nod and a smile, then blushed slightly as the other customers turned to see the recipient of the statement. Pushing out his stomach, he leaned over the glass cabinet filled with yesterday's sandwiches and dried-out cakes. The glass relented against his weight and caused the light in the cabinet to turn itself off in protest.

'Excuse me, Sir,' Coco said, with smothered giggles, 'can you move away from the glass?'

The Australian stared at her. He nodded and moved back.

Patrick threw the ice roughly into the ice machine. The steel knives screamed as they ploughed their way through the cold glass. Three customers stood around and quietly waited. One Chai, one white Earl Grey, and one slim latte. None of them had been brave enough to order the food. The bakery was late with their delivery again, and Patrick had done his best to over-apologize to each of them. The steam from the foaming nozzle filled the shop, and with the air conditioning on low, there was no room for evaporation. The nozzle's sweat pasted itself onto the glass as it slowly turned back into droplets. Patrick sharply commanded Jasmine over the roar of the ice to turn up the air conditioning, which she ignored by defiantly opening a box of readymade fruit salad laced with sugary pineapple juice. Patrick focused on his newly placed posters, he anticipated that the strain of the heavy air would force the thick paper to collapse, but it didn't flinch, and he silently admired his use of double-sided tape.

The Australian grew impatient as the previous three customers left satisfied and another five entered and were awaiting their orders. The van arrived at the back, and Coco ran out to meet it, directing the fresh sweetened pastries to the correct position.

The Australian looked up at the mask. It was a strange mask — didn't look Chinese, he thought — more Venetian. The more he stared at it, the more he thought the mask was grinning at him. He thought for a second it moved, but then Patrick started the ice machine again, distracting him.

Patrick stared at the line and counted five brownish heads, but then he saw her and her oversized black bag. His stomach leapt as his excitement grew. She was here, here! He started to worry last Wednesday when she didn't show her face. It had been over two weeks. He wondered whether he'd gone too far when he gave her coffee for free. It wasn't a big deal, and there wasn't much left in the flask anyway. It didn't cost the corporation anything if he gave out a free coffee once in a while to his valuable customers. After all, he was the manager. Yet here she was, her own tiny footsteps once again graced the place where he worked. He told himself silently to relax and finished the iced cafe latte quickly. He didn't look at her, he desperately wanted her to notice him and his skill at dispensing coffee beverages in a kind and considerate manner.

Coco arrived with a tray of pastries and placed them on the counter. She rushed behind and took the orders while Patrick and Jasmine finished off the previous ones.

'Can I have some sugar?' one customer asked, and Jasmine looked at the service table—hardly any sweetener, no brown sugar and about five white sugar packets remained in the containers. She ran to the storeroom and grabbed the nearest box of sugar to replenish the service table.

The iced latte was now nearly completed and stood proudly on the counter. Patrick stared at the Australian, who was heavily involved with his phone.

'Okay,' Patrick spoke loudly, 'here you go, sir.' He pushed the plastic cup farther out onto the counter. He decided to try and appear courteous and generous like good managers are, and he said, 'We so sorry about the wait—you take muffin, sir, they're fresh.'

The Australian stared at the sugared muffins and said, 'No thanks, not today.' He grabbed the plastic cup with his thick fingers and rushed straight to the door.

Patrick moved on to serve a tired-looking couple with ease. Although they spoke Cantonese, he thought it unprofessional to speak anything else but English to his customers, so he answered their Cantonese requests in English. He still didn't look at the small woman. He stood tall and strong, awaiting her kind, soft face. He didn't know much about her except that she was from Canada and that every Friday, she bought Chinese noodles from the old hags across the road, then came in and ordered an iced latte. Once he had enough courage to ask her whether she liked Chinese food, to which she replied, 'Yes, of course!' while looking at him with her clear, beautiful brown eyes.

He then noticed her carrying a cheap and flimsy white plastic bag, wooden chopsticks sticking out and asked her with much surprise, 'You know how to use chopsticks?'

She answered with a confused and curt 'Yes.'

He hadn't noticed the slight hostility but had smiled and nodded enthusiastically. He never had the courage to ask her whether she had a boyfriend, but he assumed she mustn't. He had seen her on and off during lunchtime when she arrived with two friends. They had sat together at a big round table chatting incessantly. Of course, he couldn't help but stare at her, he noticed her friends' movement and reaction in response to her continuous chatting. She must have a lot to say, he assumed. Her friends smiled on occasion and appeared interested, which conveyed to him even more strongly that she was perfect. Small and petite, like his dream woman would be — special, interesting, polite, and pretty without too much makeup. How his mom would praise him if he ever took her home and introduced her. He could hear her words: 'You got yourself a good girl; you take care now.' Unfortunately, she had yet to return his stares, she never turned to find his face when she had collected her coffee, never looked over at him during her lunchtime conversations when he purposefully cleaned the table beside hers.

He finished his second order and felt his excitement grow as he saw her head behind a skinny American. She's next, she's next, he repeated like an incantation in his head. He finished the order for a black coffee quickly and placed it messily on the counter. Some of the coffee spilled out onto the counter, and the American, about to voice his disapproval, stopped when he witnessed Patrick leaping to greet this girl with such a smile.

'Hello, lady,' said Patrick cheerfully, 'how are you today?'

She looked at him with the same clear soft beautiful brown eyes and the same slight turn in her mouth. She blushed deeply and flicked her roughly cut fringe in front of her eyes, a reaction to her shyness. She answered him softly with a small laugh, 'I'm good and yourself?'

Patrick, thrilled with the return of the question, clapped his hands together and released them as if rejoicing to the sounds of a song. 'I'm wonderful!' he beamed.

'Great.' she replied, she became aware of the danger of his reaction. Her eyes quickly left his as they were drawn to the mask. What a funny mask, she thought. I've never seen anything like it.

It was now time, Patrick thought. He practiced this question for the past five days, to ensure that he would say it correctly. 'Where have you been?' he asked confidently, his eyes shined through this interest.

Her eyes left the mask and she looked at him in surprise.

'Home. I went home.' she answered.

'To Canada?' he loudly announced proudly.

'Yesss.' she said. She grew uncomfortable with his familiarity. It wasn't very appropriate behavior, she thought, but at least she'd have a good conversation topic over lunch with my friends.

THE COFFEE SHOP MASQUERADE

'Can I have a black Ethiopian blend, one sugar?'

'Of course, of course,' he replied, remembering his position as manager of the coffee shop. He continued smiling at her while he poured her coffee from the readymade flask. The two expats behind her coughed into their smirks. She sensed them, turned around and met them with helpless eyes.

Patrick stood to the side as Coco took over the machine, he proclaimed loudly, unaware of her embarrassment and immune to feeling his own, 'You know, I miss you when you're not here.'

'Oh really,' she said, tightening her lip. As she turned a violent shade of red, she could feel the shade descend down her neck. It was one thing to be hit on, but it was another thing to have to deal with this new coloring. She held blushes for a long time. It would take her face an hour to calm down, and she had a meeting with her boss in 20 minutes.

'Yes, yes it true,' he nodded while acting out a poor frown, 'two weeks is a long time.'

She laughed nervously. Coco passed him a grande latte and rolled her eyes. The pale white girl pushed her teeth together silently, she prayed she'd get out of here safely. He handed her the coffee very carefully. 'What's your name?' he asked bluntly.

She saw his strong affection and turned her eyes down. 'Kimberley,' she whispered.

'Kimberley, Kimberley,' he repeated, saying the ending too fast and searching her for confirmation.

She nodded, and bit on her lower lip. She rocked her body, ready to make a dash out the door. She looked up at the mask, which seemed to be laughing at her.

Not meeting Patrick's eyes, she motioned goodbye to him, although she was sure it never left her mouth. She left quickly as Patrick stood staring at the back of her short blond hair.

'Goodbye, Kimmmbly,' he said loudly.

Her back gave a flinch, and as Andrew held open the glass door for her, she greeted him with a look of distress. She tripped over the small step and Andrew held out his hand to help her, but she miraculously found her own footing and turned to smile at him.

Andrew's eyes curiously followed her to the entrance of the outdoor escalator. He then turned and walked in, allowing the door to close behind him. Unknown to him, the breeze on which he entered had disrupted the Buddha in the window and its corner started to wilt. He walked innocently toward the counter to greet an ecstatic Patrick.

'Good morning, sir,' Patrick said cheerfully, recognizing him as the man who ordered the different samples of coffee for himself and the crazy lady. 'Can I take your order?'

7

HONG KONG ROMANCE

Don't display what people desire,
And their hearts will not be disturbed.
—Tao Te Ching

Grace had lived in Hong Kong for two years with her husband James. Recently, they'd come out of a rough patch where James admitted he was addicted to porn. Grace was devastated but agreed to go to therapy with him and since then their relationship had improved. 'One day at a time' the therapist said, and he was right. Things were getting better and they had finally decided to talk about starting a family. Currently Grace worked part-time at a fancy members-only club that claimed to *encompass a welcoming space for innovators and adventurers to convene, form connections, and unwind in the company of like-minded individuals amid unparalleled luxury and comfort.* Grace liked working there and enjoyed feeling like she was part of a community filled with 'important' people.

Today in the gym, opposite the coffee shop, Grace weighed herself for the third time. She heard her phone ringing on vibrate, lying on the edge of the counter beside the slick black hairdryers and mirrored tissue boxes. Not recognizing the number blinking on the phone, she considered not answering it, but it could be someone at work. She answered the phone, pretending to be busy, 'Yes, hello?'

She stared into the mirror, examining her face and pores, then turned to her side and looked sadly at the emerging flab rising up the sides of her jeans.

'Grace?'

It was a male voice, but she had no idea who.

'Yes, this is Grace,' she answered breathlessly, deciding to hoist up her jeans—perhaps a belt would help? 'Who is this, please?'

The male voice, disturbed by the lack of recognition, cleared his throat, 'This is John.'

'John?'

'Yes, John, James' boss.'

'Oh right. Of course, sorry.' She stopped playing with her jeans and stared into her flustered face; her eyes moved down and focused on the soiled cotton wool ball that lay on its own.

She was confused—had she promised to meet him? She couldn't remember. By all accounts, it wasn't a heavy night. They had met in the Shangri-La lobby, had dinner at the Argentina Steak House down the road, then, according to George, it had been vital that they go to the ice bar to feel the effects of minus-18 while drinking shots of vodka, then to Dolce Vita for a nightcap. Nothing excessive, but she still did awaken this morning with a foggy head. However, she could remember what had been said: they'd discussed Shakespeare, utilitarianism, and France, but nothing about plans for today.

'John, how are you?'

John replied, 'I'm good, yes, thank you, and yourself?'

'Yeah, I'm good.' she sounded tired, and she couldn't believe the scale—she didn't want to. She had never been this size. 'Well, a bit of a hangover.'

John spoke fast: 'Grace, let me get straight to the point—have you got time to meet today?'

'Umm, yes I do, actually.' She wasn't working again until Thursday. She wished she could work more; they'd promised at the interview that a new full-time position would come up soon for her, but that was eight months ago.

'Well, can we meet in half an hour?' John asked.

'Okay, sure.' She didn't know what he wanted but was sure it had something to do with her knowledge of the shops and sites in Hong Kong because that's why anyone called upon her who was visiting. It reduced her to feeling like a mere tourist guide who was never paid.

'Where do you want to meet?' She thought that she could grab a cab on Hollywood Road and meet him at the hotel.

He replied, 'At the coffee shop we passed last night.'

His answer surprised her.

'Okay, which one? We must have passed a dozen.'

'The one you said you went to often.'

'Oh, the one next to the escalators?'

'Yes, so can I see you there in half an hour?'

A local woman appeared beside her, lifting up a hairdryer. Grace noticed that her jeans were practically falling off her. She was so busy admiring her figure that she didn't notice that the woman was about to start the hairdryer. Grace lifted her left finger to her ear, attempting to drown out its numbing noise.

She spoke loudly into the phone, 'Sorry, there's a lot of noise in here. You see, I'm in the basem...'

'Can I see you in half an hour?' John shouted, loud and impatient.

'Half an hour, yes.' She looked up at the clock. She couldn't do this in half an hour. She needed to go home and try that belt on. She couldn't meet him with flab spilling over her sides. 'No, hold on, can we make it 45 minutes?'

'Fine, fine. I'll see you then. Bye, Grace.'

'Bye, John.' He put down the phone before she had the chance to say goodbye.

He could be so serious and rude; no wonder people are afraid of him, she thought. However, she always had liked him. From the first time they met, when she was nervous and talked too much, he smiled at her, honored that he made such an impression. She saw him whenever he was in town. She had to, but she didn't mind. He would invite her along to those quiet boring dinners with serious men, all too important to have any real conversations, finding that only to be a weakness. So, she would arrive and start the table talking. Secretly, she believed that she should've been hired as a party socializer.

But he liked her and ensured that he sat only one chair away from her at these events and that they had some time together to talk alone. Everyone else was afraid of him — of his position, his title — it was like they sat on broken chairs when he was around, desperately afraid of them collapsing. It amazed her that they behaved like this. He wasn't a god, far from it. From last night's conversation, she identified gaps in his general knowledge, but she admired how he dressed and his quiet power, but it didn't infiltrate her. It just made her feel safe. He was attractive, and she had noticed other women eyeing him, they noticed his wealth, and to be honest, she did have a little crush on him, but it was more like he was a headmaster, and she was a schoolgirl, but she did envy his life, how he could travel extensively and lavishly.

Unashamedly, she took a cab home when she could have easily taken the escalator up. She located the belt that she had been thinking about and saw that it did help to keep her jeans in place, she rushed out and flopped down the stairs to the coffee shop on the corner.

Her face was red from running around and her hair hadn't

THE COFFEE SHOP MASQUERADE

dried fully, but she walked toward the coffee shop, smiling at Kimberley, a girlfriend of hers, who passed by on the escalator. Waving a hello, she entered the busy coffee shop.

John looked at her, and his mouth began to run dry. She was radiant, like a bright yellow daffodil poking its head out of the graying snow. He was deeply in love with her, more than his limited vocabulary could express, the same sort of love that one writes about in books or tries to portray unsuccessfully in those soppy American movies, he supposed, for he wouldn't normally read those words or watch those awful movies, but this emotion was strong and surged within him.

Before she arrived, he had been struck by a glossy ad in *The Economist* for an expensive jewelry brand that seemed to sing to him, its image was the naked back of a woman's silhouette, her nude perfect back adorned with a thick diamond necklace, with a poet's words centered elegantly below it:

> 'You are the call, and I am the answer,
> You are the wish, and I the fulfillment,
> You are the night, and I the day.' –D. H. Lawrence

He studied it and felt the words sink deeper into his being. Perhaps he could just show this to her, this mere page, and she would understand. There would be no need for small talk, only a nod. He had made up some excuse to come over this time just to see her. Last night at dinner, her leg had accidentally touched his, and she had let it lie there for a couple of seconds. He closed his eyes, enjoying the sweltering reaction he had to it. Now, he watched her walk over to the table, he felt himself melting into the chair. She was completely oblivious of this power she had over him, and he would never admit it. Even if things did go his way, he would never let her know the extent of this turbulent powerful emotion. He could barely stand up, but he smiled, leaned his knees on the side of the table and stood tall. She moved toward him and kissed him on his aging cheeks. He had to stop himself from plunging his lips onto her neck.

'Sorry I'm late. I was just finishing at the gym when you called.' She sat down opposite him, and he smiled at her lovely way of apologizing all the time for unnecessary things. It was charming, and he viewed it as a sign of good upbringing.

'It's okay, I haven't been here long.' He lied — he had left the minute after they had spoken, wanting to get a good table for them both. 'I was just admiring the bad jazz that appears to be on repeat. I was thinking that they must have developed a system that transmits messages through the music to make you order more coffee.'

She laughed at his observation and answered quickly, 'How very Aldous Huxley of you.' She looked around, her eyes landing on Patrick behind the counter.

John, not wanting her eyes to look anywhere else but into his own, spoke rapidly, 'Thank you. Well, there's no other reason why I could've been coaxed into purchasing this disgusting Gingerbread latte.' He held up his cup as proof.

'Wouldn't that be amazing if they did do that? Imagine the scandal.'

John wished to avoid such silly conversations, moved in his chair uncomfortably, 'Yes, quite...,' He coughed.

Sensing something in his disapproving manner, she looked down at his coffee, 'Oh, I'll go and get something. Do you want anything?'

'No, no, I'm fine. I've got all the sugar I need with this artificial syrup.'

She gave a little smile, grabbed her bag, and headed toward the counter.

John grew annoyed with himself. I should've offered to buy her one — why didn't I buy her one? What sort of man doesn't offer a woman a drink? I should've stood up, I'll go up — and he was about to stand up when he saw her chatting with Patrick behind the counter. She whispered something to him and John watched as Patrick went into the back room. The music volume was lowered, and he saw her mouth say, 'thank you.' He watched Patrick smile, nod his head to the side as he giggled at something she said. *She has that way John admired, that delicious way of making you feel better about your life in a moment* — everything could be forgotten. Patrick didn't offer her a free dose of syrup, and she wasn't summoned to the small counter like the others. He gently passed the coffee over, which she graciously accepted. She said 'bye' and walked back toward John. He wished that she'd walk over, put down her drink, sit on his knee, and kiss him in front of everyone, but she didn't and sat opposite him, detaching herself from his vision.

He had left *The Economist* on the table, bringing it just in case there was nothing to read in the coffee shop. He didn't like being caught empty-handed in these situations that called for him to wait. He never read *The Economist,* but it was something a man like himself was supposed to read. He couldn't be bothered reading up on world events; he had people do that for him.

'Anything interesting in your *Economist*?' she inquired.

'No,' he said, and looked up at her, contemplating whether to show her the ad, but he wisely thought against it. It was too early — maybe later when she became more attached, 'nothing terribly interesting — same old melting ice caps in Greenland.'

He felt as if he should say something else, but he couldn't think and leaned toward her. He wanted to tell her that he longed for her, that all he wanted was an afternoon with her, but all he could say was, 'you're looking lovely today Grace.' he said it shyly, for he was never good at giving compliments. His wife always said that he said them in such a way that they seemed insincere, as if he was forced to. 'Very fresh.'

He noticed a pink tinge appear on her neck, and he wanted his fingers to go toward it, press down on it to show her that he could invoke such little sensations within her as well.

'I feel good, thank you, still a little bit hung over, and you?'

'I'm fine,' he said, as he tried desperately to pull his eyes away from her neck. 'I'm glad I left early.'

'Early? It was 2 in the morning when you left.'

'Was it really!' he mimicked her reaction. 'Well, I'm not surprised. I was so awake. I didn't sleep too well on the flight.'

She remembered one of their past conversations about one of the local guys in Shanghai who had stupidly admitted that he liked to listen to Indian music, she added, 'Watching too many Bollywood movies, were you?'

This fell flat on John. He felt himself becoming aroused again, even after the time he'd spent in the shower envisaging her with him. How could this happen to him now? He had women off and on, but he had never felt like this — never walked around carrying such weight and urges within his being, not even about his wife when he had met her, and now he had an erection again.

'Hmm?' he quietly replied, his mind hurtled deep into a fantasy. He needed to say something to stop from being consumed by it. 'Listen, I hope you didn't take to heart what I said last night about the theater. It was only my opinion, and a drunken one at that.'

Grace shook her head and looked down at the table, embarrassed. 'No, it's fine, you're entitled to your opinions. I was going to apologize myself. I didn't mean to lay into you.'

He admired her humility, as he didn't often find that within women, especially women at work, they always seemed to be out to attack or destroy his views, his work, but she inspired him to speak tenderly and honestly. 'No, you didn't at all. It's nice to have conversations that don't include the cost of stock prices…. In a way, it's nice to have someone to discuss things with. Not many people discuss things that are out of our sector.'

She looked up at him, surprised by his honesty. 'Not many people do with you, you mean. That's because they're in awe of you. The last thing they want to do is upset you and lose your respect.'

She started to shiver, as the air conditioning vent sat right above her head, and she wrapped her massive pink scarf around herself.

'Not you, however, right, Grace?' he sounded different, soft, and less like the man he appeared to be.

She bit down on her lip, not wanting to get into this, but knowing that she couldn't help but continue. 'No, I do respect you, but maybe I should be more like that. James had such a go on the way home over how I spoke to you. I forget you're his boss. Maybe I should idolize you and be like everyone else.'

'No, don't do that. It would bore me. You're more interesting than that.' He smiled and took a sip of his sweet drink.

Grace, unsure of what to say or where this was going, sat there looking out the window. She saw that it had gotten dark, and the rains were coming. She was afraid to turn to meet his eyes, for she saw that like the rain clouds forming outside, something was forming in here within him. Some darkness was beginning to settle over her, ready to saturate her. She sensed him sitting back and heard his leg gently touch the side of a plastic bag.

She looked down. 'You've been shopping?'

Brought back down to the present, he looked down at the

flimsy white bag. 'Yes, I took your advice. I got up and took the Star Ferry to Kowloon. I must say, though, you didn't warn me that I was going to be overrun with Indian men trying to sell me a cheap tailor-made suit.'

She nodded and let out a little laugh, relieved that the moment had gone; 'Really? What did you do?'

John sat up; he felt himself empowered with a new energy as his erection had started to die down. 'Well, I told them I lived here, of course, thinking that would stop them from bothering me, but it didn't. I don't think they believed me. It's simply amazing how they can tell who's a tourist and who isn't. Then I took a cab to Mongkok.'

'A cab? You couldn't take the MTR?'

'God no. I always enjoy the cab rides here — they always seem so interesting. I like looking at the masses of people walking, the people who sell crazy things on the sidewalks. It's just so real and alive over there compared to here.'

She smiled at his obvious enjoyment telling her this story. It was strange though, as if he was someone else retelling something that they had read in a guidebook buti t felt pleasant, almost like they were old friends simply talking.

She replied, 'Yeah, I know. It's the real Hong Kong. I'm always exhausted after going over there. I think it's something to do with travelling over water.'

'Possibly,' he said, nodding enthusiastically.

'But why do you never stay over there? Why do you always stay over here?' She then took a sip from her latte, which was still too hot, and she cupped her hands around it, in an attempt to project some of the heat throughout her body.

'Because I want to stay in the best hotels, especially after that tortuous flight, and the best hotels are here.'

'Yes, that's true, but the view is a lot better from Kowloon.'

'Yes, you're right.' John felt that time was beginning to run out on him, and he then decided to move forward towards dangerous territory. 'Were you surprised that I called you?'

She turned her eyes away from him. She sensed something was about to be said. She shook her head. 'No, I figured it's because you need more shopping tips. Oh god,' she decided to try and lighten the mood, 'you're not going to take James' advice and go to Shenzhen, are you?'

He smiled, 'No, no, I wouldn't do that even if I was completely drunk, let alone sober. No … in actual fact,' he took a deep breath and stared down at the emptying plastic cup, 'it's just that I wanted to ask you whether, well, if you'd be…' he said and looked up at her, and saw that her face was also bent down — did she know what was coming? '…interested in spending more time with me. I'm not here very often, and I just thought it would be nice to see more of you.'

He waited, watching for a reaction, but she didn't move, or even breathe. 'Okay, not the reaction I was hoping for.' He sat back, deflated and anxious.

'Umm…,' she gently started to come back to life, 'no, I'm sorry. What do you mean? You want me to show you around or something?'

'No, not exactly,' he whispered, desperate in his attempt not to sound sordid, 'I mean something a bit more personal.'

'Personal? I don't really understand.' Her hands now played with the plastic lid, and she started shivering again.

'Ugh, you're not making this easy for me, Grace. I mean a bit more than that.'

Suddenly, it was as if all the lights were switched off, and dark, thick rain clouds smothered the light. She felt odd and looked at her own reflection in the window. 'You want me to have an affair with you?'

He wasn't prepared for these words, and they surprised him. He sat back, unsure of what to say. 'Grace, please...,' but he couldn't deny it. He had gone this far and wanted to continue, either stop it or move it forward — whatever needed to be said had to be said now, as he couldn't live like this. 'Wow, okay, yes, if you have to be so definite, in a manner of speaking, I do.'

The full realization of the moment hit her, and she swallowed hard. She couldn't stop shivering and heard her heart beating in her ears. She felt like she was submerged in a bath filled with cold water. She tried to warm herself, rubbed her shoulders and looked toward the counter, where the staff were busy replenishing cups. She stared at the shelves, and her eyes met the mask. Eyeless, it stared back.

Such a strange mask, she thought, not like anything I've ever seen. Its color and shape vexed her — Italian, but then not. It was bizarre and not cohesive, almost as if it was hiding something underneath — some other face. Another life? Then it was as if the light came back on, and she looked at John's hopeful eyes. She didn't know what to say.

'Sorry, I just didn't expect this. I thought you called me about where to go shopping or something.'

'Oh, well, naturally, if I needed any help with that I would, but surely this doesn't come as a surprise to you, the way we talk sometimes and the way you look — or should I say, the way in which we both look at each other — the intensity. You must feel it. Listen, I'm not normally wrong about things like this. I know I'm not. You have to admit to something.' He didn't acknowledge the change in her, the shift in her body. He was too eager for her reaction — did she, or didn't she?

'Yes, I suppose,' she said. She wished she was drinking something stronger than a latte. 'I'll admit to some of it, especially the last time you were here and that night at the champagne bar.

But to be honest, I've tried to get rid of all these thoughts about you. I just never expected you to actually say any of this. I can't deny I do want to be with you.'

A master quick in the use of word manipulation in helping to determine people's meaning or to confuse them, John replied, 'You mean you can't deny you don't want to be with me?'

'Isn't that what I said?'

'No, you said you can't deny you do want to be with me.'

'Oh, doesn't that mean the same thing? Oh, never mind. Wow, I feel stunned.' She felt sick—not in a physical way, but in an emotional way, like she was walking a thin line, the razors edge liable to fall at any moment. The fact that it was from him, she did find him attractive, and perhaps she did flirt with him too much—like that night at the champagne bar, when she said she wished she had married someone more like him—of course, she was to blame, but that was just after James admitted to his addiction. It had thrown her off course, she never had suspected that she would have to deal with her husband having an addiction and drunkenly she whispered to John that she wished she had married someone like him, in that moment it was the truth. But now faced with it, she didn't know what to say.

He spoke, 'I know it may seem a bit forward, but as I only see you so rarely, I don't see why we can't indulge ourselves and have some fun.' He smiled at her. He wanted her to understand, he was willing just to have her for some of the time. Of course, he wanted all of her, but was willing to make do with what he could get—even this was better than not seeing her at all, but she didn't absorb any of his hopes.

'You don't?' she replied. She glared at him. It seemed like a game to him, a mere sport. I'll just be another notch on his bedpost.

'No, there shouldn't be any problem, as you're not involved

in my everyday life. I consider it to be a fair idea — unless, of course, you don't want any part of it.' He sat back and sighed. This was proving to be more difficult then he hoped. He assumed she would be more than willing, she had given him signs, the touch on the shoulder, the wide eyed looks of interest. Maybe this was not worth it after all.

She thought, he really has thought about this. She felt isolated and uneasy in her lack of planning. She had no one to turn to, not even herself, because perhaps through this they could both share something. It could give her a release, some secret that she could conceal, get back at James for everything that he put her through. 'No, it's not that. I'm flattered, really, it's just so ... I don't know. We only see each other a couple of times a year. You're suggesting we be together during this time?'

He was delighted with her thinking, with her appreciation of the plan — it fueled him further. 'Well, yes, it's the only suggestion I can come up with — unless, of course, you can think of anything else?'

Reality soon arrived as the rain outside the windows began to drip down the glass. 'Umm, no ... but to be honest, isn't this a bit quick? I mean, you hardly know me.'

'Of course I do, or at least I know all that I really want to,' he answered honestly. He didn't think he could know any more about her — it would only push her further into him, and then he couldn't see himself functioning without her.

'I don't know.' She looked at him sadly, still unsure of what he had in mind. Was it just sex without love or emotion, and was that even possible?

'What is there to know?' He put up his hands, weighing the decision, 'You want it or you don't.'

That irritated her, his casual simplification of the matter. She always thought that if she was to have an affair, there would be monumental attraction, and the man in question would be Italian or French, his language filled with broken English and tempting kisses. It would only last something like 12 hours, and no one would ever know. She never expected to share this with someone so obviously a slave to such precision. 'Well, so much for romance.' she had to say it, 'aren't these things supposed to develop naturally?'

'Well, they could, then nothing might happen for years. I'm taking the initiative here. It's quite simple.'

'I wouldn't consider this situation simple. In fact, I think it's rather far from simple, especially as we're both married to other people. What about guilt and the consequences of being immoral?' her biting remark startled him like an electric shock felt from touching cheap fabric.

'Really?' he started to retaliate. 'Why on earth are you bringing up morality and guilt? Grace, people have been doing this since time began.' He then stopped himself from expanding, as he could see that it wouldn't do him any good to undermine her. She was too strong. That was what attracted him to her, so he thought it might be better to switch off quickly and see how she reacted to being blinded like a moth when the light goes out. 'Maybe this was a mistake. I thought maybe you'd be ready for something like this.'

'Ready for something like this?' she spat out the words with distaste. Obviously, he had underestimated her state.

He saw her anger seep out and retracted, 'I didn't mean it like that. Come on...'

'You'd be ready for something like this? Is it like a secret society that I've come of age and am now ready to join? I have to graduate into an unhappy self like you to be ready for this?' She finished, breathless, and thought that it was best that she should just get up and go, but she looked out at the vicious rain and heard laughter from the people who had just entered, ridiculously drenched. It was safe in the coffee shop. She saw his fuzzy reflection in the window; it looked sad and hurt. Ugh, she thought, as her compassion grew. Who was she to judge and say those things, and here, amongst the dark skies and whirling air conditioner, he appeared like a little boy, lost and hurt. She took his hand, 'I'm sorry, maybe that was a bit too much.'

Inspired by her touch, he said, 'Grace, it wasn't my intention to upset you. Listen, it's only an idea I wanted to run by you. You don't have to make a decision now.'

'I don't know — it's all very weird. This time last year, I'd have jumped at this, but now I'm happy, we're happy. I don't know if I should disrupt all of this for a few days with you.'

'It's not a few days, only a couple of hours.' He gently stroked her hand and wished it was her naked back, but after he saw no emotion, he sighed and let go of it. 'Okay, but there's nothing else to say then.' He didn't want to let her go, but he was too great a man to sit there and beg, even if he did love her.

Suddenly, she spoke fast, 'No, wait. Let me consider it. I'm just afraid, and a bit miffed. I never thought in a million years you'd ever want me like this.'

'Well, I do,' he said, quickly he reattached his hand to hers.

'No, I mean that you'd have the courage to confront me and ask me like this. It's just so formal.'

'Grace,' he said, now becoming the powerful man he was, 'if I want something, I get it. It's there if you want it. Just don't keep me waiting for too long.' He then kissed her hand, and as he bent his head over, she saw that he still had the majority of his hair. He then stood up and reached for his jacket.

'Where are you going?' she asked, surprised.

'I'm jetlagged. I want to sleep.' He looked out into the rain and decided to take a chance, 'You can join me if you want.'

Seeing Grace curl up again into her scarf, he added quickly, 'Okay, sorry. That was tacky. Well, I'll be seeing you for dinner. You can give me your answer then.'

'What, in front of everyone?'

'No, Grace, ever heard of the adjective 'subtlety'?'

And there it was. He made her feel like a schoolgirl again, unaware of what she was saying. 'Oh yes, of course, sorry, I'm just nervous. That was stupid of me.'

'Hmm, anyway, I'll see you then…' He walked toward the door, then remembered something. He returned to the table. He saw that her eyes were deep within the realms of shadowed secret thoughts, his voice shocked her and jolted her to sit up.

'Well, I might as well give you this in case,' he said, then dropped a black plastic key card on the table, its gold, elegant lettering smiled up at her. It fell on top of his *Economist*. 'That is, if you come to your decision earlier. My room number is 1802.'

'Thanks,' she said. She didn't know how to reply but felt that it was already decided.

'Okay, well, you know my position. Please don't delay any further than you have to on deciding yours.'

She stared up at him. 'It sounds like we're negotiating a deal.'

'Well, we are, in a way. See you later.'

She watched his face scrunch up as he prepared for the rain. He left the coffee shop. Luck ever present with him, the rain started to let up, and he managed to get a taxi to stop.

Grace watched as a strange-looking man wearing a tight suit—Monkey— bumped into him, and John pushed him back. Monkey fell on the road and swore. John ignored him and got into the taxi.

Monkey got up and brushed himself off. He was very hairy and dark and he walked past the coffee shop, slowly looked in— his eyes met Grace's. She turned away, as she felt he was dangerous and looked toward the mask. It was no longer there.

She sat back. Did I imagine it? Did I just imagine all of that? Even that strange mask? Was that a warning?

But then she stared down at the black hotel key.

Patrick walked over to her with a tray of small cups. 'Grace, do you want a free sample?'

She nodded at his polite sweet face, 'Sure, Patrick. Thanks.'

When she looked out again, Monkey was gone and the strange mask was back on the shelf.

8

Jasmine's Choice

On tiptoe: no way to stand.
–Tao Te Ching

Jasmine didn't like the mask. From the moment she'd had seen it in the storeroom, she'd wanted to throw it away. It gave her an odd feeling, like something malicious was associated with it.

Coco said it was bad luck to just throw it away: 'It could be haunted, then the ghost will be angry and come and get you.'

Jasmine was about to say that she didn't believe in those things, then suddenly, all the lights went off in the shop, and Coco giggled and whispered to her in the dark storeroom, 'See, I told you. Better be nice to the mask.'

It was three days before the full moon, and Jasmine ignored the mask that now sat on the shelf behind the counter. If she did look up, and it caught her eye, she would turn her head away quickly.

A male customer stared at her, he had just asked how old she was. She grinned back shyly. Finally, for once, she voiced internally, it's me who is noticed.

Male customers normally tended to cavort with Coco, her friend and work colleague. Jasmine assumed it was because she was prettier, with her short, fashionable haircut and bold blond highlights. Finding Coco's confidence intoxicating, Jasmine often surrounded her like an admiring child, trying to absorb her essence and cursing her own almond eyes, so plain. Her chin was her father's, odd and pointed, and her nose was flat. Her head was laden down with thick heavy hair that could do nothing else but hang like a horse's tail. Jasmine unconsciously hid away, curling her shoulders like wilting petals, often petrified that anyone should want to interact with her in the coffee shop.

She desperately wanted to raise her head and look over at the counter to see if Coco or Patrick had noticed this interaction, but she found herself staying still. Keeping her head safely down, she stared hard into a black smudge on the floor that had been left by a stranger's shoe.

She finally answered, 'twenty Two.'

'Do you like working here?' he inquired.

She nodded, trying to hide her smile. She managed to tear her eyes away and look toward him, but not at his sweaty face full of anticipation. Instead, she settled her eyes on the great mass of gray hair that sat upright on his head, making her wonder if it was real.

'Do you like coffee?'

This question caused her to bend over and shake violently with silent giggles. She wanted to reply, what sort of a question was that to ask someone who worked in a coffee shop?

'Perhaps I could ...' he stumbled over his suggestion, 'well, perhaps you could join me sometime for a cup, somewhere else maybe?' Looking around with his right eyebrow lifted. He almost released an audible 'tut' at the shabby decor in which she had to work.

'Somewhere a bit more up-market?' he suggested.

She stopped moving, not understanding what he meant. Up-market, like Kennedy Town? Or Mongkok? She wondered.

Taking her silence to mean interest, he said, 'What do you say? I want to talk to you about something.' He reached out to touch her elbow.

Immediately, she jumped away, alarmed by the threat of a real touch, a real gesture. She wasn't used to being touched except by Coco and occasionally by her mother and sister as they grabbed her roughly and poked fun at her.

'Well, maybe some other time.' She heard him say with disappointment as he climbed up the small steps toward the red couch.

Jasmine stood still like a figure encased in marble, ridiculous in her pose. She felt the mask peer at her, scrutinize her, like her mother and sister did.

She thought of what it would be like to be with someone like him — a Western man, with his enormous stomach and rich clothes. She imagined that he lived in one of those posh residences with 10 doormen and a man in the elevator — a grand apartment with an incredible view of the island that would make her feel smaller than she already felt, an apartment on the 60th floor, somewhere in the sky with the birds. A place her grandfather would have said wasn't fit for us mortals, not even in our big planes — only for nature's creatures and the spirits. He had said many things similar to this. He had been there when they ripped down the magnificent colonial buildings of the past, replacing them with mirrored steel and dull concrete. *'Moving on to keep up,'* is what he remembered from one of the government posters placed around the city to keep morale up. *Keep up with what?* He wanted to know. He had said they raped Victoria Harbor, taking her sleeping sediment from the water to make more land. He had said that it wasn't natural and that they'd have to pay for it later, that the earth wouldn't let them do this without a fight. Nature and the gods were in control, not man. Her mother would tell him to shut up, sit down, and stop frightening the children, but he would ignore her defiantly.

'They must know,' he would shout, pointing at her and her older sister as if they were to blame. 'There will be consequences for all this movement, consequences.'

That's what he always said. Normally, after his daily declaration, he would leave them for the afternoon and visit his old friends in the park. Jasmine followed him sometimes and watched him circle the lifeless park with other men who were all the same height, bent over like dying blossoms from working in the fields or at the harbor. Some of them had been shipped over from the mainland at the expense of their guilt-ridden children to enjoy their retirement in the luxurious sanctuary of the islands.

Jasmine watched them talk in small groups. They looped the park endlessly like scrawny sparrows. Now and then, one would laugh out loud, and the others would smile with broken teeth, but her grandfather mostly remained serious, deep in thought — maybe contemplating more opinions to announce to us over dinner, Jasmine had considered. She wanted to ask him so many things, like why he was so serious, why her mother cried at night, and where her father was, but she dared not. Instead, she had kept quiet and still, like the old, thick Chinese furniture crammed into their little apartment. Sometimes when she came home from school to the empty flat, she often hid in the ancient chemise that her great grandfather brought over as a wedding gift. She would sit snugly within its wood, comforted by the homey smells of well-cooked rice and vinegar while using her small fingers to trace the organic scratches that lined the doors.

THE COFFEE SHOP MASQUERADE

A young woman touched her softly, bringing her back to the shop. 'Have you any more stirring sticks?'

Jasmine nodded, 'I get some now, okay? You wait?'

'Yes, of course,' the young woman replied.

Jasmine ran into the storage room and picked up a long, thin cardboard box. She scratched the tape open, which forced her to look at her nails. They looked weak and sad. I should go and see them at work—this evening, she thought.

Her mother and sister ran a manicurist business together in Tsim Sha Tsui. It was in a small, dark room on the third floor of an old building that appeared almost derelict. At street level, there was a very loud Australian bar and a sex shop. From the outside, a poorly painted kangaroo with tattered boxing gloves highlighted the bar's theme. Inside, the walls were littered with boomerangs, cork hats, didgeridoos, and poorly painted dreamtime murals depicting various fictional bush battles with Bunyip's.

'The owners aren't even Australian,' her sister once said, 'they're Indian. Imagine opening an Australian bar, and you aren't even Australian.'

No one answered her when she said it. Her sister didn't like foreigners. The few foreigner customers they had always went to her mother.

The sex shop below was constantly busy. It didn't feel the need to darken its windows for the modesty of its customers. Wire racks filled with marked-down erotic films sat chained outside its entrance. Inside, one could see dildos, costumes, massage oil, and strange boxes filled with beads. Jasmine didn't know what else was sold in that shop. She was too shy to venture inside, but she always tried to get a glimpse through the window or door. This had encouraged one of the young men at the door to tease her by attempting to entice her in, knowing full well that her family worked upstairs.

Jasmine had never wanted to work with her mother and sister. They tried teaching her their trade, telling her that it was her job to help and support them and that she would learn it quickly, but she failed. Her hands were often warm and became sweaty easily, which irritated the customers. She could never fully reach the grit under people's nails without stabbing into their sensitive skin. During the first few weeks that she had worked there, it grew harder to survive under the watchful eyes of her mother and sister. It was enough that they had to live together in the same small flat that she had grown up in, but to sit every day and argue over which channel to watch and what tea to drink to lose weight made life tedious for Jasmine. Dangerous thoughts had entered her mind that involved electrified train tracks and blunt stones, but she learned to shun them by purchasing more childish furry toys.

Lying on her bed, she would stare into an audience of *Hello Kittys* — sweet porcelain dolls — and *Sesame Street* characters that she bought regularly, finding comfort in their blank smiles. Her mother finally noticed her lack of interest one time when Jasmine became so distracted by the local news and the impending arrival of Giorgio Armani that she painted the wrong color on a client.

Once Jasmine noticed, she tried to remove it but knocked over the bottle of polish onto the customer's skirt. It was only a Giordano skirt, but the girl demanded money — a lot of money — as compensation. There had been shouting and disappointment, and Jasmine was marked as a disaster, the shame of the family. If she couldn't paint nails, what else could she possibly do?

After two weeks of cleaning up clipped nails and dried skin, she succumbed to her mother's suggestion to go to temple to ask for help. She found the courage to venture out on her own after one of the Western customers had mentioned that she had lovely hair. At the temple, she bowed graciously with her offerings and tried to arouse her own mind to receive whatever was suggested, but nothing sounded. She waited a week until the suggestion came in the form of the local newspaper.

Her sister saw the ad first.' Why not this? You can make coffee—you always make good tea,' she had said in a rare moment of kindness. Jasmine looked at the words, *'assistant in Soho branch.'* Soho on the island! She immediately felt excited but was quickly brought down after her mother had laughed at the idea.

'You think you can carry hot things without dropping them? You can't! You're a clumsy, stupid girl.'

Her sister shook her head. 'Mama, be nice, she needs to try something else. Remember what you said?'

Their mother looked down and nodded. 'Okay, but do not get too upset if you don't get the job, okay?'

Jasmine nodded.

She had gotten the job from Patrick after he observed how neatly she folded her jacket and placed it on the back of the chair. She then decided to pop in and visit her mother and sister once a week in the nail parlor, always bringing them stale pastries from the shop, which they devoured, then complained about.

She would let her mother examine her hands and tell the other customers in the vicinity that her daughter worked too hard. 'Look at these poor hands serving coffee. Too many people drink coffee nowadays; that's the problem with the world—bad stomachs.' Jasmine allowed her to moan, praise, and complain while she sat silently, scanning through the new mainland magazines that they received once a week.

Her sister would look over, envious of all this attention, but then she, too, drowned out her mother by watching the local game show that was on every evening at five, always chewing the latest seed or dried fruit to encourage weight loss.

Back at the coffee shop, to the young woman's relief, Jasmine reappeared with the box of stirrers.

'Thank you,' she said, as Jasmine offered her first choice out of the box.

She replenished the stand, while still feeling the male customer's eyes on her, his stare invigorated her, it caused her to stand tall and confident, but then she recalled her own beliefs and quickly tried to extinguish any more wistful thoughts of him and what he could give her.

Nothing but trouble, she heard her mother's words from inside her. Those men, only dirty Thai or Philippine whores end up with those men. Not many good local girls would lower themselves. She admired her mother's thoughts, she genuinely believed that Westerners were inferior to the Chinese, a thought she inherited from all her grandfather's daily sermons.

Jasmine returned to the counter, it was unusually quiet, she watched Patrick wipe down the coffee machine. She noticed him move his hands over the black mantle machine with care, as if he was rubbing a delicate lamp when what it needed was a good scrub. Jasmine bit down on her lip, unsure of what to do next. She could still feel the mask behind her as if it was watching her.

'Hey, Patrick, did you put the mask here?'

Patrick shook his head, 'Not me. Must have moved on its own.'

'Do you think it's haunted?'

He looked up at it and smiled. 'Probably, isn't everything old haunted? It could explain why I keep finding cups in weird places.'

'What do you mean?'

THE COFFEE SHOP MASQUERADE

'Our cups they keep moving around the coffee shop. The other day I found one in the fern and then two in the staff toilets. Then yesterday I was making a macchiato and I swear I put down the cup and was foaming the milk and when I turned to pour it in the cup had disappeared. I looked around and thought, what am I going mad and then suddenly I saw it, do you know where it had moved to?'

Jasmine shook her head.

'Right there in front of it.' Patrick laughed and pointed to the mask, 'it was as if the mask wanted it's own drink.'

Jasmine looked up at the mask and shivered. 'Maybe we should give it a coffee every day, you know like an offering?'

Patrick stared at her. 'Yeah, maybe that's a good idea.'

She watched him make a single espresso and place it in front of the mask.

'Now then mask, how do you like that? No more funny business, okay?' he said smiling.

Jasmine gazed at the mask and suddenly she heard her grandfather's voice, "Give a man a mask and he'll tell you the truth." She felt a cold quiver run throughout her body and she cleared her throat. This mask doesn't belong here, she thought, such things belong in forgotten boxes, hidden away. She shook her head and looked out into the coffee shop. The customers sat mute, as they turned magazine glossy pages and sipped on sweet milky coffees. Those who sat with others stared into their beverages or out through the smudged windows. But it was all so quiet and calm. Such a noontime hush was peculiar, and Jasmine felt unbalanced. There was no noise, nothing to do. The counter was clean, and there were enough ceramic plates and cups.

Suddenly, a couple of local schoolgirls rose from their chairs and laughed together as they hurried out of the shop. Jasmine jumped to action; she rushed over to their table to clean it. Their two empty cups contained neatly folded biscotti wrappers. Two stirrers were lying across one cup like a cross, with a torn, full sugar packet balanced on them, its thick body ready to fall off at any moment. Jasmine grabbed the cup's handle and tried to balance the arrangement all the way to the counter. Successful in preserving the display, she placed the cup down gently and showed it to Patrick, who didn't react and merely dumped the rubbish into the bin behind the counter. Jasmine returned to the table to wipe away any crumbs. She then saw that a message was written on the table, which had been hidden beneath their display. It read *'Fuck Sandra'* in black biro, written in polite, standard handwriting.

Jasmine knew what it meant, but didn't know any Sandra. As she tried to wipe the obscenity away, she found that the pen ink came off, but the message had been scraped deep into the pinewood table in biro. Such precision for such an ugly word. She looked up to see whether Coco was around but couldn't see her. Patrick was busy with three returning customers. At a loss for what to do, she rubbed it again and tried to lessen the vulgarity of its appearance. She allowed her finger to feel across the letters. They felt coarse, causing a thin red line to appear on her index finger.

This marking had aroused a different feeling compared with the scar that she had felt along Coco's back. That scar had felt alive. It was raised, long, pink, and had minuscule lines that resembled an earthworm up close. It went the whole length of her body. Jasmine pushed her to explain what happened but Coco had relented and said it was from an accident that she had when she was a child. Jasmine thought it strange that Coco chose to stay silent, as most people loved to relive such stories. However, Coco appeared to be embarrassed and almost ashamed.

It was in a drab department store in Mongkok, where they

had gone after the cinema one day, after holding hands in the dark during a movie about love, that Coco had revealed her scar to Jasmine. They shared a changing room as they tried on T-shirts with the friendly faces of Cookie Monster and Elmo on them, delighted that they could still fit into children's sizes.

'What is that?' Jasmine said without thinking.

'Nothing.'

'Can I see? Please?' Jasmine said, she was desperate to keep the intimacy between them.

Coco didn't answer but raised her T-shirt to reveal the full extent of the line. It was almost perfectly diagonal, it started under her left shoulder blade all the way down to her right hip. Jasmine was shocked by such a horrific line, and she touched it and let her finger follow its path. She could still recall the emotion, the sensuality of being able to feel this intimate part of Coco. She became excited and wanted to explore it, to permeate her deeper, to follow the lines, the movements of her body, her tiny breasts. Jasmine, lost in rapture, was ready to divulge that she wanted to lower Coco's jeans so her finger could move down, but she was stopped as Coco lowered the T-shirt. They bought the T-shirts and never spoke of it again, but Jasmine still thought of that moment, of that line, of the ache she had.

As Jasmine rubbed, the words didn't disappear but only seemed to grow clearer and stronger. She looked up again toward Patrick and caught his eye. She pointed to the table, distressed, and he rushed over.

'Did you do this?' he whispered angrily.

'No, of course not, it was those school girls. They must have done it. They covered it up with their cups.'

He didn't reply and chewed the inside of his mouth — the way he did when his mother entered the shop in the afternoons.

'We could cover it,' Jasmine suggested.

'With what?'

'A flower or plant.'

'You!' he said harshly. 'You always talk of flowers and plants. I said no. The company says no. We can't afford fresh flowers every day. This is a coffee shop, not a restaurant. Flowers give the wrong impression.'

Jasmine looked down again at the words, which seemed to gleam at her. *Fuck Jasmine*, she thought they should read. Everything that she suggested, Patrick ridiculed or ignored. She normally didn't say anything to him directly, preferring to let Coco answer or shout at him. Remaining quiet, she watched Patrick stare down at the words until two new people entered the shop, he then left her without a word. She was afraid that he wouldn't return and that she would have to guard the table all day to stop anyone from sitting at it.

Coco re-entered, and Jasmine called her over.

'What is it?' Coco said, as she tenderly touched Jasmine's arm.

'This.'

Coco read the words and started to snigger loudly, most patrons in the coffee shop looked curiously towards them. Jasmine, aware of the unwanted attention, tried to quiet her.

'What should I do?' she whispered loudly.

Coco, fell onto one of the table's chairs, and giggled further. Jasmine smiled at her, happy that she was amused, she knew they would laugh over this later. Patrick walked over to them, furiously. 'Get up!' he shouted.

Coco didn't and started to chuckle louder at Patrick's order. This enraged him, and he shouted at Jasmine, 'Take this table away into the storeroom. I'll have to get it fixed.'

Jasmine tried to pick up the table, but its heavy iron legs proved too much for her.

'Help me,' she asked the amused Coco.

'No, leave it here.' Coco replied, grinning.

'No, I can't—it's not right.'

'Oh, don't be silly. It's all right. Anyway, it might be a secret message for someone, and if you remove the table, then the person will never get the message.'

'But it says,' she stumbled, unable to bring herself to say the word. 'But it says …' She carefully pointed at the obscenity. 'It's not a nice message.'

'No, but it could mean something else, couldn't it, like a request or suggestion?'

Jasmine realized what Coco was insinuating and started to snigger.

Patrick called for Coco to return to the counter and help him serve the four people who were waiting. She walked off with a sly smirk.

Jasmine was left stranded once more with the table. She studied the words. Maybe Coco is right, and it's some sort of message. She sighed and watched Patrick and Coco serve the customers, who stood around them like intimidating dark shadows while they observed their drinks being made. She watched them both beat the espresso machine, rinse the filter, and warm the milk. Each was trying to outdo the other, and it caused the scene to become turbulent and nervous, almost as if something frightening was going to happen, like a humongous wave was about to wash over all of them, swallowing them all up as it made its way up the hill.

Then someone touched Jasmine on the shoulder. It was him again, the male customer.

'Here,' he said, his hand carrying a card. 'I wanted you to have this in case, you know, you change your mind or something.'

Jasmine looked down at the pristine card. She saw his name. It was Rob, Rob Busch. She took it, unable to say anything.

'That's my mobile number.' His pudgy finger clumsily tried to point out the tiny line.

'You can call that if you want to chat.' he talked confidently and normally, as if he did this every day, leaving Jasmine embarrassed. She wasn't like this—she never even looked at Western guys and didn't find them attractive. Sometimes her eyes would follow Coco's when she pointed out a good-looking guy or drooled over Hollywood movie posters, but Jasmine could never see it the attraction, the lust over some stranger whom she never found handsome.

Anyway, her sister always said that Western men drank too much, that they were too hairy, and always got huge bellies when that were old. They expected women to do things for them, sick things in bed, she said. 'You could just tell by looking at them,' she remembered her sister had announced as they walked along the Avenue of Stars. 'I mean, look at all those DVDs and sex shops—they're always filled with Western men. They're sick.'

Jasmine nodded in timid agreement, although she wanted to note that it was normally young local men who went into the shop next door to the Australian bar. Sometimes it was young Asian women. Jasmine would stare at them, bewildered, wishing she had the courage to stare into the face of ecstasy. However, she didn't say anything to rival her sister's opinion.

Jasmine took the card and started to shake.

Rob mumbled, 'I hope to hear from you soon.'

She swallowed her shame and didn't look up to see whether anyone had witnessed what had occurred. Instead, she took to walking around the shop collecting empty cups and wrappers.

Reaching the red couch, she picked up Rob's cup and suddenly felt nauseous. She tried her best to appear busy, shielding her scarlet face, but she wanted to cry, and felt as if she could sob for hours. She heard Coco laugh out loud and looked up, curious

THE COFFEE SHOP MASQUERADE

to see what was so amusing. It was Andrew, the good-looking guy with the headband again. He had been in twice today already, once for a latte, then water, and now again. What for? She watched Coco flip her short hair as she smiled, elated that he was speaking to her.

Jasmine was already aware of Coco's crush on him and watched them enviously. She almost lost her footing as she walked down the small steps. She knew that Coco wasn't really laughing — she was only pretending, flirting, being artificial. She only really laughs when she's with me. What sort of a man is he anyway, with his headband and those shoes? He looks like he should be shut up in the Po Lin Monastery on Lantau, like that Monkey character whom she often saw when she took out the trash. He sat on the roof opposite the coffee shop, dressed in his costume. Thankfully he never noticed her, and she would carefully stare at him as he sat drinking cans of beer. Some people just aren't suited to modern life, she thought. She looked up at the mask — it looked back at her like it was laughing.

Jasmine decided not to move toward them, but purposely took an awkward path past them to the left and around the counter. She deliberately wanted to avoid Coco's gleaming eyes. She looked down at Patrick, who was bent over trying to scrape up the remains of a chocolate muffin that had slipped off the counter and been trodden on.

A cough from the counter called Jasmine to attention. A thin Western woman waited to be served. Jasmine stepped over Patrick to reach the counter's slim opening. Jasmine nervously remembered that Patrick didn't like her to serve because he said her English wasn't good enough, but she suddenly felt empowered. She wanted to ignore Coco's delighted squeals and so she became someone else. 'Yes?' she greeted the tired-looking woman.

'Yes, hi, umm, I was wondering if you could help me. I'm working with *Island Mag*, and we're doing a piece on all the shops and restaurants in the Soho area. I contacted your head office and mentioned coming in to take some pictures and perhaps conduct a small interview with some of your staff for our website.'

The woman spoke fast, and Jasmine, was unable to comprehend everything she said, and started to blush. 'Um, not sure.'

'Are you Jasmine Wu?'

'Yes, how come you know my name?'

'Well, the head office gave me the name of the manager. Are you the manager?'

Patrick immediately popped up from beneath the counter. 'No, I'm the manager. I'm Patrick.' he said and presented his hand over the glass jar filled with plastic cookies.

The woman tried to reach it but missed and ended up awkwardly shaking his fingertips. 'Well, hello, Patrick, but the head office said that Jasmine Wu was the manager.'

'Yes,' Patrick replied unfazed, 'but I am.'

'Yes, well that may be, but I think I really should deal with Jasmine. After all, they gave me her name.'

Patrick became deeply immersed in explanations about what the head office had failed to do. He didn't sense Coco creep up on the conversation.

'What's going on?' she asked.

Jasmine replied, 'The head office gave the wrong name to this woman. They said that I was the manager.'

'Really?' Coco said. 'Well, why don't you call the head office, Patrick, if you're that concerned.'

The woman became agitated at being at the center of such petty confusion. She was only there to take some photos and get one of them to say something nice about the area. She looked relieved at Coco's suggestion. Patrick rushed off to the storeroom to call someone while Coco started to serve the people waiting behind the woman.

Jasmine stood still, not knowing what to do.

The woman looked at her. 'Well, do you mind?' she said, pointing to the camera that hung around her neck. 'I'd love to take a photo of you, some in here and some outside.'

'But I not manager.'

'I know, but you work here, and they did give me your name.'

'Okay,' she said softly, not wanting to cause any more unnecessary trouble for this woman. She walked toward the front and stood at the window. 'Where?'

'Well, how about at that table? If you could carry a cup over to it ... yes, just like that.'

The camera seemed to mimic Jasmine as it clicked nervously. Those who were waiting for Coco to complete their coffees watched the stilted photo shoot.

The woman, sensed Jasmine's embarrassment and asked her to go outside, where she told her to sit on the crooked concrete steps.

'Yes, that's perfect, Jasmine,' the woman said. 'No, don't look at the camera. Now look at the camera. Yes, don't smile too much, easy. Yes, like you're happy, but not excited.'

The woman shot photos, and Jasmine sat there, amused. A couple of strangers passed by and stopped to watch, but Jasmine didn't think of them as the woman began to throw compliments at her. After five minutes of shooting, the woman stopped and walked over to her.

'You know you really are beautiful. Have you done modelling before?'

Jasmine shook her head.

'You should you know — you have a special look.'

Patrick threw the door open and hit Jasmine on the back.

'They want to talk to you on the phone,' he said breathlessly. 'Please, this way, Miss, this way.'

The woman rolled her eyes at Jasmine as she followed Patrick inside. Jasmine walked back into the shop and over to Coco.

'Well, what happened?'

'Nothing, she took some pictures, that's all.'

'Did she say that I should go next?'

'No.'

'Did she say anything?

'She said I was beautiful,' Jasmine replied, quietly.

Coco pulled back her head, surprised. 'She did?'

'Yes, she said that I should be a model.'

Coco snorted. 'What? You a model?'

Jasmine looked down and didn't reply.

Coco pushed past her roughly and walked over to the cake fridge.

The woman came out and apologized to Patrick, who now seemed like a gracious host, he asked her, 'You need to take more photos?'

'No, I don't think so. I think the ones I took are perfect.' she said, grinning over at Jasmine.

'But that only Jasmine. Perhaps better all of us. Yes, okay? And one with me alone. I the manager.'

'Okay, if you like.' The woman sighed and looked over at the fresh coffee that waited to be consumed.

The three of them stood together: Jasmine, unable to smile; Coco trying to present her best pout; and Patrick grinned, his arms tightly locked around the two of them, as if they were best friends and loved working together.

The woman took one shot, and then one of Patrick on his own. He put his hand on his hips like Jackie Chan and pushed his groin forward. Jasmine looked at Coco, expecting them both to share in a giggle, but Coco hurried away.

Jasmine was fearful that Coco was angry with her, and she looked around the coffee shop, eager to occupy her mind with distraction. She saw that Andrew sat at a table, busily tapping at his phone. The woman who had finished taking photos of Patrick motioned for Jasmine to come over. Jasmine followed her toward the door and noticed that Patrick had given her a free coffee.

'I wanted ...' the woman whispered, looking back at the counter, 'I wanted to give you my card. You see, I have many friends in fashion and perhaps they might know someone whom you should talk to.' She handed over her card to Jasmine. It felt flimsy and light, like standard paper that came out of a home computer.

'Well, just in case. Also, some of the photos might come out well, so send me an email, and I'll send them to you, okay?'

The woman touched Jasmine's shoulder, making her feel instantly sleepy. She then mouthed 'bye' and left the shop.

Jasmine turned and watched as Coco moved toward Andrew, probably to tell him what a stupid lady that woman was and how she told Jasmine she could be a model — imagine that. Coco stood there talking to him, but Jasmine noticed a silence as he returned to his phone, but Coco didn't leave. Playfully, Coco moved her legs, waiting for him to entertain her more, but then his phone rang, and she departed, crushed. Jasmine met her eyes and smiled sympathetically; she hoped this was all behind them now.

Coco picked up her head and beamed at Jasmine as if she knew full well that Jasmine's eyes would meet hers. Excited, she rushed over to her. 'He's so cute,' she said, animated. 'Like Ryan Gosling, but better, don't you think?' She expected a nodding agreement to come from Jasmine, but she didn't say anything —

she found that she just couldn't.

'Oh, what now? Don't give me that look. What are you angry about? What I said? Come on, you know you can't be a model. Your mother would never let you, and what about me? What would I do without you? We're like sisters, remember? Even more than that, we're like soulmates.' Coco said soulmates in English, which seemed to demean its importance, this caused Jasmine to remain mute.

Coco attempted to embrace her like a small child, with one arm circling the other. She sensed the interaction's awkwardness and Coco became hostile.

'What's wrong now? You think you're all that now 'cause some skinny, ugly Western woman said so? She isn't even a proper photographer, you know, not for fashion. She can't even take shots right. You were standing too close to the light, which will only make the photo blurry,' Coco said, confident in her ignorance of photography.

Jasmine didn't react and started to pick at her nails like she did when her mother and sister scowled her, awaiting the loud words to pass.

'I know about these things. Don't forget my brother is a photographer, a professional.'

Jasmine grew irritated. She met this 'professional' photographer, who agreed to take pictures of her for her social media pages—posed images that would appear effortlessly stunning, she hoped. Jasmine wanted them to be taken using a soft backdrop in a studio, but he had insisted on taking them in broad daylight on the harsh wasteland outside his tower block in Tung Mung. The backdrop to her photos was now a concrete wall washed in graffiti that cited the names of local gangs and the faded canary high-rise buildings that acted like dirty screens in the distance. They appeared to have no windows, only ghostly frames. In this severe wilderness that connected the tram throughout Tung Mung's surrounding areas, Jasmine had stood in her bright-yellow gingham dress and white high heels, with her hair down. Posing sweetly while holding the pink handle of her favorite *Hello Kitty* bag, she had stood awkwardly as he shouted directions at her viciously.

'Move left, leg out, don't smile, look down, don't smile.'

He made her look like an abandoned doll left to break down and ferment in the overgrown weeds and pebbles.

She wanted to cry when she first saw the images. Coco talked about how powerful they were, how her brother was on his way, a real artist, even though he only worked in a small electrical shop in TST.

'They really showcase a statement,' Coco said. These words were too large and foreign for Jasmine; she only nodded politely and paid the $500 without realizing that she was the only client who had ever paid for his time. She wisely decided to leave them off her social media pages and kept the one of her taken outside of Ocean Park when she was 8 years old and dressed in a bright pink tracksuit.

'My brother would have said something if he thought you were a model, and he didn't. Actually, he said you were hard to direct.'

Jasmine felt someone looking over at them, and she tried to quiet Coco down. It was Andrew, and Jasmine nudged Coco.

'He's coming over.' she whispered, delighted that she could change the subject.

Coco excitedly hopped over to the counter, believing he wanted to make another purchase, but he didn't move toward her—instead, he headed toward Jasmine.

'Excuse me, I just got a message from my aunt; she's visiting and said that she left a white plastic bag with some souvenir shopping in it. Don't suppose you found anything like that?'

Jasmine shook her head. 'I'll check storeroom.'

She rushed in and found one of the evening staff taking off her jacket. It was the strange plump girl who never spoke to anyone from the day shift. Her name was Ruth, her face was covered in strange piercings, and her hair was half black and half blue. She didn't turn to see who had walked in, and Jasmine decided to do what she always did and ignore her. She felt along the table to find the lost-and-found box. It held some keys, a hotel key card, and a pale gold necklace that was made of fake gold, according to Coco.

Jasmine returned defeated, looking more upset than him.

'Well, if you find it,' he said, passing her his card, 'can you call me?'

Jasmine nodded, and read it: *Andrew Green, Journalist*, with *SCMP*'s proud letters in the corner.

'Okay,' she replied.

'Thanks.' he said. She expected him to leave, but he didn't, he just stood there transfixed. Jasmine immediately looked down at the floor but failed to see what had grabbed his attention.

'You okay?' she asked anxiously.

'Yes,' he nodded, 'just dizzy.'

'Sit down.' she said, grabbing his arm. She helped him over to an empty chair without realizing that it belonged to the table marked with the obscenity.

His face pale, he looked down, spotted the curse, and smirked. 'Don't see much of that here.'

'What?'

'Graffiti, defaced furniture.'

'Do you want water?'

'No, I need to breathe, that's all—too much caffeine, I think.' He let out a small laugh.

She watched him exhale through his nose, which made him look ugly, then she felt Coco behind her.

'What's wrong?'

'He isn't well,' Jasmine whispered.

'Are you okay?' Coco said, bending down to so she could touch his knee.

He nodded and looked up into Jasmine's concerned eyes. 'You're very beautiful,' he said, almost unaware of what he was saying, as if he had no choice about what came out of his mouth.

Jasmine returned the compliment with a gracious, shy smile.

Coco huffed and stormed off.

'And very kind,' he said bashfully which caused Jasmine to turn red. 'I should go.'

He grabbed his bag. Now that the words were said, he finally felt free of them, as if someone else spoke through him. He rose, not looking back.

Jasmine turned and headed toward the scowling Coco and exhausted Patrick. The mask caught her eye, and she stared at it, from somewhere inside of her, a voice sounded, *beautiful Jasmine, as intoxicating as the white blossoms. Time to find balance.*

She shook her head — how odd! There's something in that mask. She went over to offer some assistance to Patrick and Coco as the coffee shop got busier, but their self-importance took over and she decided to leave them. Her day was ending.

She walked back to the storeroom and to Ruth, who stood with her eyes transfixed on the broken coffee bean clock. Jasmine saw that she was chewing bright yellow gum.

She still felt the effects of the compliments and decided to be friendly and smile at Ruth as she headed over to her locker. From her pocket, she took out the three name cards she had received that day and started to study them carefully.

'How many did you get?'

Jasmine jumped at the sound of Ruth's voice. It was quieter than she imagined it would be.

'Oh, three.'

'Three's not bad for the day.' Ruth said, and she got up and walked over to her. 'Can I see?'

'Sure.' Jasmine handed them over.

'Oh yeah, I know him. The fat guy always wants an iced macchiato, and that guy, he's pretty good-looking, not bad. Who's the woman?'

'A photographer. She came in today to take photos of the coffee shop, she said I was pretty, maybe I could be a model.' Jasmine replied like it was a ridiculous joke.

Ruth nodded. 'Cool. Well, you could you know. Anyway, you don't want to be here forever.'

'Why? It's okay.' The idea of not working in the coffee shop never crossed Jasmine's mind.

Ruth snorted, 'Is it? Working with those two? They belong here — you don't. All they do is compete over making coffee. Coffee! Like who gives a fuck?'

'Where do I belong?' Jasmine asked quietly.

'I don't know, but not here in this place, you know…' Jasmine watched as Ruth's eyes stared up at the clock. 'I normally get an average of eight name cards a night. I have his, but not his, that reporter guy, he's pretty reserved.'

'I'm not into meeting guys at work.'

'Oh, right, mama's girl, huh?'

'No, just not into that.'

'Okay, it's only a bit of fun is what I was going to say — don't take it so seriously or else you'll end up like those two out there.'

Ruth held the back door open, and Jasmine watched Patrick and Coco race to complete their final orders. It was weird as if she was really seeing them for the first time.

THE COFFEE SHOP MASQUERADE

'So sad! Anyway, I'm on now. See you around, Jasmine, right?'
'Yeah,' Jasmine said. 'What's your name?'
'Ruth.'
Ruth left and Jasmine stood up, feeling like another wave was coming, except this time, she was ready.

9

A Chip in the Cup

Good people do not quarrel.
Quarrelsome people are not good.
          –Tao Te Ching

Charlotte and William had been in Hong Kong for four days. They were staying with their nephew Andrew in his apartment on Robinson Road on the 33rd floor. After this trip, they would go down to Singapore and spend the hot humid days hiding from the sun visiting war memorials and searching for William's great uncle's name. They wouldn't find it, as he'd lied to the family about where he was during the war.

Today, Charlotte and William sat on the red couch. It was raining, and they're both in foul moods.

'What's wrong now?' William asked.

'Nothing,' Charlotte snapped, pushing the cup away.

'Are you going to be like this the rest of the day?'

She didn't answer but stared down at her pale suede shoes that were now freckled with damp spots. It had rained every day since they arrived — worse than London — and she was sick of it.

'I apologized, Charlotte — there isn't anything else I can say.'

She sniffed as she focused on two small men who entered the

coffee shop laughing heartily, their little bodies jiggling along to their thoughts.

William stared at her face, watching for any opening — a raising of her eyebrows, a twitch of her mouth — but she remained defiant, passive. He collapsed back into the red couch, defeated.

'There's a chip,' she said suddenly.

He sat up immediately. 'What?'

'I said a chip in the cup.' Her voice raised in volume.

He peered over and looked into the blackness. He couldn't see any chip around the edge, but he decided not to argue. He picked it up and without acknowledging her walked over to the counter.

She watched him walk — strong, head up.

They had been coming to the coffee shop for the past three days. He had taken a liking to it and didn't want to brave any of the local shops she suggested. He ignored her when she pointed them out to him — the small shops with different names. She wanted to say to him, 'How can you travel and not try new things?' However, she didn't. He would just sulk. The airline magazine had promised that she wouldn't be short on choices, as culinary experiences to be found in the city were endless. However, she had not found it so because since his operation, William didn't like to try new things. He would say, 'You never know what you're getting.'

He still has some presence, I suppose, she thought, watching him. *Not much, but there's something about him.* It was something she never had been able to define. She remembered him walking toward her when they met one night in town before they were married. She stood on the corner trying not to appear nervous. He smiled and picked up his pace when he saw her. Handsome, so handsome — a bit too handsome, her mother had cautioned. She had shivered then in anticipation, keeping her fingers tightly wrapped around her handbag strap as he walked up to her. Her future then seemed exciting and alive within his affections for her. She hated that she romanticized him — she always did this — making him out to be more and better, but often when faced with him, she immediately became disappointed and embarrassed by her own thoughts.

She watched him find Jasmine's eyes and explain the chip in the cup. She could tell from her enlarged eyes that he was using complicated English. *Why does he do that, constantly over-complicate things and use language that a girl like that wouldn't understand?* Jasmine looked at him, smiling and nodding, concerned. She attempted to search for the chip with her fingertip, but didn't feel it, so she passed it back to him, shaking her head.

Then more words passed between them. Charlotte could not hear them, but she watched as he grew angry, raised his voice and stood up taller so that he could talk down to the petite, pretty girl. Finally, Patrick intervened, apologized, and replaced the cup with a free refill. She watched him return, shaking his head. She saw the manager grab Jasmine tightly by the elbow and shout at her in their own language. She didn't see how Jasmine reacted.

William walked back to the red couch triumphantly, like he used to walk before he became old. 'Here.' He placed down the fresh cup.

She mouthed 'thank you,' and they sat once more in silence, and watched those around them come and go.

He started to attack his pastry with a knife, but it failed to cut through the sugar, so he attacked it with his hands.

'Funny seeing little men in here, isn't it?' she asked.

Taking that as a sign that all was forgiven, he said jovially, 'Yes, yes it is. Do you think they're part of a circus?'

'Yes probably. They look like performers.'

'Probably Disney.'

'Yes, that's right.'

'Well, what do you want to do today?' he asked her cautiously.

She waited before answering, trying to decide whether she should let go of this anger so quickly. Normally, she'd drag out such remarks for a few days at least to make him aware of her hurts, sadness, and underlying disappointment that seemed to swell beneath the surface like a blister ready to burst. He wasn't immune to saying mean things, foolish things that rolled off his tongue before he knew what they meant. Being too proud a man, he wasn't able to excuse them but swallowed them whole and then defended them.

She ignored him, picked up a piece of the pastry, and chewed on it slowly.

He turned his attention to the floor.

Last night's comments distressed her still. They were embedded in her now like a sore that would not heal, for he had said it, and it never could be unsaid. Last night, she hadn't slept and wound up lying awake in the small IKEA bed and listened to the air conditioning trying to produce cool air that came out tepid. She wished she could hear the city's traffic, people talking, something to take her out of her thoughts, but she couldn't. Andrew's apartment was up too high, nothing surrounded it, only silent air. The birds didn't even venture up that high. The view from his flat seemed to rotate. This had been very exciting for them when they first arrived in the city, but after three days, she wanted things to stand still. Her senses felt numbed..

When she walked at street level, she was forced to absorb the city's chaos—loud squawks, phones, TV commercials in the middle of the road, and the smell of grease and garlic. Even at the tiny beach, the sea annoyed her as it noisily stroked the shore. The parks were odd and artificial, everything appeared streamlined even the trees with nothing truly established, the lack of real nature rattled her. She hadn't felt like herself since she arrived. There was nothing but what the island kept through its inhabitants' limitations, and the incessant rain smothered everything and destroyed hours of their precious time.

After three hours of turning in the bed, suppressing her sobs, and reliving her meaningless life, she finally persuaded herself to get up and walk around the apartment as quietly as a ghost.

Thankfully, she didn't need light, as the surrounding buildings shined brightly through the windows. She looked out onto the city's sleeping silhouette as she curled up on the marble windowsill and rocked herself. She found it chilly and took one of the large towels from the bathroom and draped it around her shoulders.

It's cold here. No one said it would be cold.

She had looked down at the marble windowsill, almost expecting to see her reflection, but instead saw a small feather sitting beside her. She wondered how it got there, picked it up, and brushed it against her skin. She loved feathers as a child, collecting them, keeping them safe at the bottom of her parents garden. They had aided her during her childish spells. She had wanted to be a witch when she was a child and believed she had powers, as the moon and the wind seemed to follow her. She smiled, remembering how she believed she could make the trees move and the wind tickle her neck like a loving parent. She wondered now what happened to all those glass bottles and feathers she collected. She couldn't remember why she stopped believing she was a witch. *I wish I still believed it now. He doesn't even know that about me.* She held herself tightly, happy that he didn't—she still owned that part of herself. She felt she had given him everything as a tradeoff for his affections and loyalty.

I wish I could go downstairs and disappear. She imagined herself taking the elevator down, walking the streets, seeing strange things like the man dressed as the Monkey King—how he stared at her as if she told him something awful when she hadn't muttered a word.

She let her tears take over and cursed herself for the day she had said 'yes' to him all those years ago when he asked her to be his wife. What a life—an existence stuck with someone who never wanted to marry her, which he actually said out loud: *If I was your age, Andrew, I would never get married.*

She never returned to bed. Her mind stayed awake, reliving incidents from their marriage when she wanted to leave him but found it hard to recall images. She enjoyed being married to him for the most part, which made the incident all the worse. She loved his voice, which resonated and stimulated her own vibrations. His voice had the ability to arouse and caress her. Sometimes she wanted nothing more than to listen to him and encouraged him to read to her like a child. She would lie beside him, secretly marveling at how he sounded his letters, reveling in the pleasure of knowing that this was all she needed.

Her thoughts suddenly turned to the day before, when, for a few hours, it stopped raining, and they decided to take the peak tram. When they arrived at the station, they quickly discovered that everyone else had the same idea, and the line was long and fat. He grew angry at the rude tourists pushing and pulling beside them, and upon entering, he had left her to try and get a seat as fast as he could. When she finally got on, he stood up and pointed down to the bench, 'Over here.'

She sat down and waited as the tram jerked and pulled them up the hill. She could almost feel the pressure of the rope about to snap, and she had grown anxious about their possible imminent death, but the feeling passed, and she relaxed into the weight of gravity, focusing on the view outside. Finally, she could see green apartment blocks with windows into strangers' bedrooms.

She then heard a gasp and turned to see what it was, with several people standing up, trying to look out. She also stood up. There was a momentary break in the crowd that allowed her to see it — the city's silhouette, magnificent in the daytime, impressive and majestic. Then the moment was lost as others blocked her vision with snaps from gurgling cameras.

'We're on the wrong side,' she had said to him as she sat back down, but he never answered her.

When they reached the peak, they could barely see the city, which was encased within clouds and pollution. She could see some apartment buildings and a line of green, but the buildings sat behind a screen of clouds. When they lined up to return down the hill, she wondered how many would sit on the right side this time. When they were allowed to enter, people once again pushed and rushed. She felt him poking her, and once again, she sat on the wrong side. *Is that my fate — always being on the wrong side?*

Andrew awakened early and walked into the living room, he startled her. He apologized, and they both laughed.

'Just watching the dawn,' she said.

Seeing that she was still upset, he said little, but nodded, smiled, and explained how the fancy coffee machine worked.

'I have a breakfast meeting.' he muttered, then left quickly.

That's just what she needs, she thought, still sitting on the ledge. *Another excuse to rattle me further.* She thought about her sister-in-law and her weak husband. It was enough that they had Andrew when she had no one, no child, because they came from a time when adoption wasn't fashionable, and doctors were unsympathetic to her condition. The emotion of being unable to have children, let alone enjoy the act of conception, wore on her now, as it sometimes did when it came surging forward, destroying her illusion of control. She masked this by attending various events locally with women her own age, always alert to the mention of grandchildren and sons and daughters. Most of the comments she found were mostly negative about their offspring, and she found comfort in not having any of her own. 'You're the lucky one,' a woman had said to her. 'Children and their own children are nothing but trouble and worry—it never does get any easier.' This forced her to leave these events abruptly and return to her garden, which was filled with flowers that she could help blossom.

———∞———

Back at the coffee shop, she sighed, annoyed at herself for being like this, for keeping the tension alive. But she couldn't let it go and let him off so easily. Wasting another day in the city that promised so much, she cursed the rain and herself. Her eyes wandered to the mask behind the counter—*Ugh! what an ugly thing! It doesn't look like it belongs here.*

And then something strange happened, as if someone jolted Charlotte with an electric force. She suddenly felt empowered, she sat up and looked around as if she was seeing everything for the first time. A strange voice spoke inside of her—*come now, witch, show me your power.*

She focused on Jasmine moving around the shop, collecting plates and cups, and noticed that she balanced them clumsily on her thin arms. *She isn't fit to lift plates for such a young girl—what is wrong with her?* Then their eyes locked, which caused Jasmine to lose her footing and trip on the back leg of a chair. The plates and cups exploded as they hit the floor, the sound vibrated throughout the room.

Charlotte didn't jump up to help, but sat satisfied, feeling like she had caused this by distorting Jasmine's own rhythm. She wanted to scream at Jasmine without knowing why and pull her hair hard. Jasmine, seemingly able to hear her thoughts, looked over at her anxiously as she fell on her knees to the floor. Strangers jumped up either to depart or help.

'So sorry,' she muttered before Patrick rushed over to shout at her viciously in their own language. Jasmine's face scrunched up, and she burst into tears.

Silly girl, the voice sounded inside of Charlotte.

'My, my,' Charlotte said to William, 'that's silly. All she did was drop some plates—she doesn't have to cry like that, silly girl.'

William coughed. 'She was crying before.'

'What?' Charlotte turned her head, and suddenly felt the force leave her. Her body relaxed, and she swallowed—she was thirsty.

'She already was crying while she was collecting the plates.'

'Was she?' Charlotte asked him with hostility, annoyed that her power was gone. She sat up trying to re-enact it and glared at him. 'Noticed her, did you?'

'Charlotte, don't be silly.'

'Don't you tell me what to do! Looking at her, were you? Admiring her?'

'Charlotte, that girl is crying because of you.'

'Me? I didn't make her drop those plates.'

'No, but you complained that there was a chip in the cup, and when I went over with it, her boss shouted at her for making coffee in that cup.'

'Well, there wasn't anything I could do about that.'

'Of course there was—there was no chip.'

'Yes, there was.'

'No, there wasn't—you were just trying to make one of your points.'

'What points? What was I trying to do?'

'Charlotte, you know what I'm referring to.'

'No, William, believe me, I don't.'

He sighed and hung his head.

She wanted to continue, but Jasmine's loud sobs stopped her.

'You know,' she started, 'you made it perfectly clear last night how you felt about being married to me.'

Not raising his head, he said, 'Lotte, I was only making conversation.'

She laughed and wished for that strange internal force to return. 'Making conversation? In front of Andrew? The whole thing was embarrassing to him and me. Making conversation? Perhaps, dear, it would be wise if you didn't make such conversation in the future.'

'Lotte, don't talk down to me — you know how I hate it.' His eyes, serious and alive, met hers.

She continued. 'Is that so? Well, it's obviously not the only thing you hate.' She then turned away, she wanted to cry, but she bit down hard on her inner cheek. *No more tears. I'm not going to cry anymore.*

'Lotte, I love being married to you.'

She snorted, surprising them both. 'Really? You didn't say that last night.'

'I don't need to say it to you — you know I love being with you.'

He reached out his hand, the same hand that had wiped away the thousands of tears that had fallen on her face — tears forgotten but absorbed into her being — the same hand that had embraced hers whenever she felt nervous.

She moved away from his hand. Angry, she turned to notice Jasmine still crying and picking up the broken pieces. She also wanted to cry — cry like a child, sit there on the floor with her and collect cheap crockery, but she couldn't. She swallowed her tears and wished to attack William and herself further.

'She would make a nice wife for you.'

'Lotte, don't be ridiculous.'

'No, she would—young, vibrant, fresh. She'd probably love you, a rich old sugar daddy to take care of her.'

'Charlotte, stop it!'

'Oh no, but wait—you'll never marry again, that's right, but something tells me you'd marry her in a heartbeat, that is, if she wanted an old man like you.'

He didn't answer but sat there defeated.

She felt there was more, as if she was about to peak, and she started to shiver.

'Nothing worse than an old fool. You can see plenty of them around here, can't you? This city is littered with them, stupid old men thinking that their young brides are going to bring them happiness.'

He waited for her to finish, then said, 'What I meant last night, Charlotte, was that I'd never get married again. I didn't say I never wanted to marry you.'

The night before, they dined with Andrew at the top of the Shangri-La. Noticing the fourth chair was empty, the conversation turned to marriage and why Andrew wasn't. Was it even necessary anymore? William said, after much wine, that it wasn't, that he wouldn't marry again, and that if he were young today, he would never marry.

Charlotte was appalled, excusing his silly behavior in front of Andrew and blaming it on jet lag, whispering to him, *he doesn't know what he's saying*.

William heard her and became angry, 'Of course I mean it, and I hope you'd feel the same way. Marriage doesn't exist anymore—it's too old-fashioned.'

Andrew had looked down into his glass and drank the

remains quickly.

The two of them didn't speak, but merely glared at each other while Andrew got up unnecessarily to get the bill.

On the way to the taxi, William tripped on a raised stone, causing him to fall into the ornate Japanese garden. Andrew and one of the hotel doormen rushed over to help him. Charlotte stood back, numb.

'Auntie Lotte, can you open the taxi door?' Andrew asked.

She did and watched as they placed him gently into the car. Andrew sat beside him, and she sat in the front alongside the driver without saying anything. At the apartment building, she opened the car door and let Andrew help him. William's elbow was grazed. He had hobbled into the lift like a child. She stood back and let the lift take them up. Finally, she was alone. She wanted to leave, to escape into the city and disappear, hide out in a hotel free from him, but one of the building's doormen came out and pointed to the free lift. He walked toward her when she didn't move.

'Please, Miss, the lift is waiting.' Suddenly, a wind picked up, curling itself around her, it empowered her. She smiled at him and headed to the lift. The apartment door was opened, and she walked in to find William on the guest bed and Andrew on the phone. She started to remove William's clothes. His eyes opened watching her; he didn't say anything. The wine had gone to his head.

Andrew walked in. 'I tried to call a doctor, but there's a long wait.'

'He doesn't need a doctor. Do you have TCP and some bandages?'

Andrew nodded and disappeared. By the time he returned, William was snoring heavily.

Andrew passed the liquid and cotton wool to her.

'No, no need, it isn't that bad, just a bad scrape. There will be a nice bruise there tomorrow. I don't want to awaken him. Let me have the bandages.' She undid them, cut off two large pieces, and placed them on his elbow and knee.

Andrew watched her and smiled. 'I forgot you trained as a nurse.'

She smiled at him.

'Will he be okay?'

'Yes, he just needs to sleep it off, that's all.'

They left the room, and she gently shut the door.

'Auntie Lotte, I'm sorry, I didn't think about the wine. I didn't think it would affect him like that.'

'Don't worry, there was nothing you could do — he just gets carried away sometimes.'

Andrew smiled, relieved. 'I hope you aren't too upset about it.'

'No, I'm not, it was the drink talking.' she sighed.

'Yes, yes, of course.'

'Well, I think I'm going to make some tea. Do you want any?'

'Yes, please. I have to finish off that article.'

'Oh, yes, sorry we kept you out so long. You go on and finish it, and I'll bring in your tea.'

In the kitchen she felt as if she had been crying for hours. She made the tea sweet and milky, and brought it to Andrew. She watched him type away, viciously determined like William used to be.

'Thank you.'

'No problem.' She looked down at him and felt herself wanting to hold him, hug him, and unburden herself, but she stopped, feeling like a fool.

'I'm going to watch some TV. I hope that's okay.' She always found it a little difficult talking to him.

'Yes, of course, you know how to work it?'

'Yes, I do.'

'All right, Auntie Lotte.' He said, 'Auntie Lotte,' like he used to when he was a child, awkwardly, as if it was inappropriate for him to be informal with her.

She sat and watched a horrible crime drama about the rape and murder of a teenage girl. She never watched that sort of thing normally, as she usually was too tired at night and went to bed early. She found it sickening but was compelled to stick with it and find out who did it. Watching it until the end, she was surprised to find out it was the girl's social worker, the images and conversations alarmed her.

Andrew walked in and shyly said 'good night.' She looked around the room and saw the small pieces of home that he had taken with him—the photos, the books. She began to envy him and his life, but quickly stopped herself, happy that she wasn't young anymore, that she didn't have to relive such moments and hardships.

Being a woman wasn't any better now than it was when she was young, no matter what they say. In fact, she thought it was worse now, with all the demands that were now made on women in terms of clothes, work, children, and sex. She thought about the book she had been reading on the plane—on the woes of modern-day life. She picked it up after reading the blurbs on the back that said it was 'entertaining, a laugh-out-loud modern take on modern life.' Thinking it was worth a chance—after all, it won a grand literary award—she started reading, but quickly became confused by the characters' ramblings—people who didn't appeal to her—and the descriptions of their sex lives, language, and drug use. *Is this really modern life? Reality?* The book annoyed her, but she couldn't put it down, curious about what would happen. However, halfway through, little had happened, and she thought about giving up, something she rarely did. *No wonder young people are more depressed, reading rubbish like that,* she thought.

Now faced with him and her own modern brawl in the coffee shop, she watched William tense up and hold his breath, a common feature she knew well that demonstrated he was ready to defend himself to her at any cost.

'Yes, you did,' she attacked him further. 'That's exactly what you said, that if you were young again, you'd never get married, that you regretted it.'

'No, I didn't. I didn't say that. I said that if I was young now, I wouldn't get married—there's no point.'

'Yes, because being married to me was so awful.'

'No, that's not it, and you know it.'

She turned her head to the counter and stared at the mask. Its colors were so unusual—*it wasn't meant to look like that,* she thought, and tears fell solidly. She felt the mask watch her, mock her—*some witch you are.*

She pictured herself going over to the mask and putting in on, another face, anonymous, another life —*a weaver girl, a witch who drew a line, a divide. Love but it came with a cost, sacrifice. Always at the price of the woman.*

'Damn you, Charlotte.' William said, getting up.

'Damn you?' she suddenly screamed after him, 'damn you for this life, for no choice.'

The shop fell silent, as Jasmine stopped collecting the broken china for a moment, afraid to look toward her.

Then the cake fridge let out a moan, and Jasmine started to collect the broken pieces again, keeping her head bowed. William didn't say anything and walked toward Jasmine. Picking up a piece of porcelain that was hidden under one of the small tables, he passed it to her. She was sniffing, but her tears had stopped. He bent down and said something to her, something that caused her to smile. He then rose again. The two little men also walked over to her, carrying small fragments of splintered china. They placed them in her bucket. They spoke to her, and she started to laugh. The shop appeared to be calm again.

Charlotte sat breathlessly she watched as the action in the room continued – some people left quietly, just as others, unaware of what happened, arrived. William stayed with Jasmine and helped her pick up splinters. It was as if Charlotte had never shouted, her words sliced up by the increased frequency of the fan. Had she even spoken? Her heart still beat rapidly, as the adrenalin rushed through her veins. Charlotte felt ashamed as the small men started to giggle with William and Jasmine.

I'm a fool. She wished herself back into her garden with her soft, delicate flowers that neither hurt nor provoked her. She noticed a young woman enter the coffee shop with wet hair, her face red and clean. Hadn't it stopped raining yet?

William returned to Charlotte and sat opposite her on the small stool. Inspired by his kindness, he asked, 'Well, what shall we do today?'

She looked at him and shook her head. Her face was blotched, but her eyes were vibrant. She swallowed and let the rage sink.

William said, 'Why don't we go to Disney?'

She laughed out loud, grateful to be able to release her emotion. She laughed so hard that small tears formed in the inlets of her eyes. She felt as if she was on the verge of crying hysterically. He sensed her reaction and leaned toward her, his knees touching hers.

She replied, 'Why not? I'm so bored of markets, temples, and buildings. Let's go and have some fun.' She smiled at him, unable to speak for fear of exploding into tears, so she took his hand and did what she always did—she concealed herself. She looked at the mask as she walked out the door—*I guess it's easier to wear a mask sometimes than to fight against the truth.*

10

Rob's Mission

Knowing others is intelligent.
Knowing yourself is enlightened.
  –Tao Te Ching

Rob had met Monkey a few times—twice by the pier of the Star Ferry and once on the peak. All of those times, Rob was going through a difficult period, and Monkey would magically turn up and hug him like an old friend.

'No need to be afraid—Buddha has plans for everyone,' Monkey would say and then they would go for a drink. They would sit somewhere outside, and Monkey would tell Rob rude jokes about the Jade Emperor and all his wives. Rob would relax, feeling himself realign, then they would part ways.

Today, Rob finished a meeting at the bank and made his way to the coffee shop. However, he saw a young couple with a small child enter before him and decided not to go in. Never comfortable when young families were around, he thought about going home, checking his emails, and falling asleep.

As usual, he hadn't slept much the night before, when he'd watched the dawn arrive and seen the old man in the building opposite him open a small window and stretch out his limbs with the grace of a dancer honoring the new day. Upon hearing the sighs from the docile buses, Rob felt sleepy and collapsed into bed for a few more hours, never longer than four, as this kept his mind protected. Not enough time, he had figured out, to go into painful memories, but just enough to keep him functioning.

He thought about the bank. They were, as always, concerned, unable to understand Rob's motives and tried to persuade him not to purchase that property on the water for such a lavish idea.

'You can't take those sorts of risks nowadays—people just won't pay the money,.' they'd said.

'People can pay what they want to pay—that's the whole point. I want them to value it for themselves,' Rob had replied.

This had caught them off guard. Not used to hearing such things, they worried about him and also about what the people of the island would make of such a venture. It was dangerous, silly, and would never make a profit, they said. However, the property would always maintain its value, and they could always retain that if necessary, so they smiled at him and said, 'We admire your commitment to the project, and we're willing to support you for a year.'

They'd tried to entice him to do more with his investments, but he was good at distancing himself from all their talk, confident in his venture. Upon leaving, he'd smiled, winked at the small secretary, and wondered whether she could be of any use.

He walked past an old man sitting in the small enclave of an empty shophouse on Staunton Street. The man looked tired, sitting over his small carpet filled with cheap Chinese porcelain. His eyes followed strangers, and his mouth was toothless. Rob had seen him many times. Sometimes he forgot about him, but when he remembered, he always offered him a smile, but never thought about buying anything from him.

Today, Rob stopped and said, 'You okay?'

The old man grinned, his mouth black, and his left eye glazed over by a small fog that led Rob immediately to assume it was a cataract.

'You don't need anything?'

The man reached down and grabbed a tin cup. Rob fished in his pockets for change but had none.

'Sorry, mate, but how about a drink? Tea?'

The man nodded his head and laughed as he pointed to the coffee shop.

'Ah, okay, I'll get you tea. Yes?'

The man nodded and watched as Rob bumped into a group of loud Western women carrying shopping bags.

'Sorry.' He muttered. The women ignored him, too engrossed in a conversation about childbirth.

Rob crossed the road and found a brief gap in the flow of people coming down the escalator. He opened the door to the coffee shop. The air conditioning hummed loudly, it was cold, Rob started to rub his bare arms. He saw Jasmine and Ruth behind the counter, they were laughing, but immediately stopped as he made his way toward them.

'Oh, hi,' Rob said, unaware that they were trying to avoid his eyes. 'I thought you only worked nights, Ruth.'

'Well, obviously not,' replied Ruth, stone-faced.

Jasmine quickly ducked under the counter.

'Well, okay, can I have a tea? Like, a Chinese tea.'

'A Chinese tea?'

'Yes?'

'What's a Chinese tea?'

'You know, a green tea or jasmine tea.'

Jasmine stood up and looked up at him, and he smiled over at her, 'Oh, hi! How's it going?'

Jasmine looked down again and pretended she was still searching for something.

Ruth continued, 'Well, which one, green or jasmine?'

'Umm, I don't know — you choose,' he answered breathlessly. He enjoyed interacting with these girls, especially Ruth, who had spirit like himself.

'Okay,' Ruth answered. She reached over and grabbed a tea bag without looking at it.

'Thanks.'

'Anything else?'

'No thanks.'

'You on a diet or something?'

'Me? No.'

'Okay.'

'Why'd you ask?'

'Cause you normally have a macchiato and a muffin, that's all.'

'Oh, right, gotcha. Nah. Well, this tea is for an old man outside who wanted a cup of tea.'

'So, he just asked you for tea, and you got him one?'

'Yeah, sure, well, I didn't have any change to give him, so I asked whether he wanted anything else.'

'Okay,' Ruth said, she rolled her eyes.

'You know, it's a great feeling to do someone else a service.' He handed her his coffee cup loyalty card.

Ruth nodded and took Robs the loyalty card.

'Makes you feel better, you know.' Ruth gave him back the loyalty card. 'Oh, here, you haven't stamped my card.' he said, giving it back to her.

Ruth stamped it heavily. She handed it back to him, and tilted her head to motion for the woman behind him to come forward.

Rob moved graciously; he eyed the woman.

She was young, but her skin was covered in a dark shade of makeup, making her look cheap. He felt himself wanting to say, 'Hey, love, you know that's not good for your skin,' but he watched her fumble with her money as if she didn't have enough. He was about to offer to buy her the coffee.

'Sorry,' the girl said. 'I still can't tell the difference between the coins.'

Rob noticed by her accent that she was Australian.

'It's okay.' Ruth smiled at her.

'You're Australian?' Rob asked.

'Yes.' the girl answered, irritated.

'So am I.' Rob said.

'Uh huh.' the girl replied, rolling her eyes.

'You live here?'

'Yep.' the girl kept trying to grab Ruth's attention.

'Yeah, me too.'

'Great.' she said quietly.

'What do you do here?'

'I'm a makeup artist.'

'Wow, really?'

'Yeah.'

'That's amazing.'

Rob's enthusiasm for her job made her smile, and she made eye contact with him. 'Yeah, it's okay.'

'You like living here?'

'Yeah, you know. How about you?' she asked back.

'Me?' Rob, not used to being asked anything about himself, only by his therapist whom he spoke to biweekly swallowed hard. 'I'm, well, I'm on a long vacation.'

'Lose your job?'

'No.' He laughed out loud, which caused the girl to stand back. 'Well, kind of, yeah.'

Ruth interrupted them. 'Here's your coffee and your tea.'

'Thanks, Ruth,' Rob said.

The girl grabbed the coffee and went to the condiment counter to get some sachets. Rob followed her. 'So, you live around here?'

'Yeah.' the girl said.

'Me too, over by Kennedy Town. How about you?'

'Wyndham Street.'

'Cool.'

'Well, I better go, have a photo shoot to get to.'

'Sure, yeah, hey, what's your name? I'll look out for you in the mags.'

'Sophia.' she said softly.

'I'm Rob,' he said loudly.

Sophia quickly walked out, and Rob called out after her, 'Nice to meet you, Sophia, see you around sometime.'

Sophia never looked back as she scrambled out the door. The others in the shop stared at him. Some felt embarrassed for him, others felt pity, but a few of the young schoolgirls giggled at his loud voice and enormous stomach.

Rob didn't feel their stares, their judgments. He'd become impervious to caring about what others thought about him. At first, he had thought it was some odd side effect of the medication—the antidepressants he had been on for the past three years. Once a great advocate of drugs, he had stopped taking them about a year ago, feeling ready to see the world as it is. However, the world looked different—he was altered. Maskless, he felt free again, but not like he expected. There was a freedom in how he approached life, people, things, as if everything that used to matter had now lost its value, and now he found himself devoid of that which once seemed appropriate. Things that once had meant so much—like how he looked in his clothes, his watches, his cars—he simply no longer cared about. Sometimes he would hear strange phrases come out of his mouth or truths that once upon a time he would've concealed and laughed about menacingly with a mate. These phrases now flew out of his mouth without being controlled. He didn't care — he just was, and that was that. His mom would've slapped him for the outspoken remarks, but it didn't bother him if people became upset or offended. He couldn't change how he was, not now, and he didn't feel the need.

Rob felt the tea get warm in his hands and grabbed some sugar just in case. He then shouted over to Ruth and Jasmine, 'See you later, girls.'

They didn't reply.

He left the coffee shop and headed toward the toothless man. He bumped into Harry, the man who gave him a foot massage once a week.

'Hiya, Harry, how's it going?'

Harry smiled at him, 'Oh, Mr. Rob, I'm very good and you? You looking happy today!'

'Yes, I suppose I am,' Rob replied. He liked Harry, he told him things he never told anyone while he let Harry push down on his lazy muscles. He didn't know how much of what he said Harry understood, but Harry always smiled, then Rob continued on with another story that revolved around himself and his family. Rob enjoyed his enthusiasm at rubbing other people's legs like it was a noble vocation. He didn't even mind Harry telling him he was too fat. 'Need more exercise — you no good.'

'I'm happy, and you, Harry?'

'Yes, I'm good. I won money!'

'You did? Congrats.'

'Yes, Mr. Rob, I won $10,000.'

'What!?'

'Yes, at horse racing.'

'Wow! Well done, mate.' Rob gave him his hand, and Harry shook it limply.

Harry grinned. 'I'm lucky today, and you also. I feel you're lucky today.'

'Oh, I don't know about that.'

'No, you have lucky face.'

'Thanks, Harry.'

'What's that? More coffee?' Harry laughed out loud. He often told Rob not to drink so much coffee. 'Bad for your stomach, make it big,' he would say.

'No, it's tea.'

Harry stopped laughing. 'Chinese tea?'

'Yes,' Rob nodded.

'Can I see?'

Harry looked into the water that now was turning dark. 'Good, but not buy here, too expensive.'

'I know, Harry, next time I won't.'

'Okay, Mr. Rob, but I go back to work now, see you Tuesday?'

'Yes, Harry, see you Tuesday. Hey, enjoy the money.'

'Yes, the money, $10,000.'

Rob watched Harry hurry away, laughing at his windfall. He smiled, happy that his friend had been rewarded so greatly.

He could see the old man's legs stretched out as he rushed over. Careful not to spill the tea, he bent down to him with great difficulty. His body weight was hard on his knees. He passed the toothless man the tea.

'Here you go, mate.'

The man smiled again and let out a laugh, which sounded like a sob. The man examined the plastic cup and opened it to see the tea. He smelled it, then passed it back to Rob.

'No, for you.'

The man pointed to himself.

'Yes, you.' Rob nodded.

The man smiled, nodded, and mumbled something Rob

couldn't understand. Rob got up. He bowed his head and headed back to the escalator. He was about to head down when he saw Ruth rush out of the coffee shop holding a phone. She looked frantic.

He ran over to her, 'Are you okay?'

'No, a man has collapsed. We've telephoned for an ambulance, but I can't see them.'

He saw that a crowd had gathered in the shop, and he entered. 'Okay, everyone out,' he announced, loudly.

Everyone left, and he was alone with the young father who quivered on the floor. He had already been rolled over to his side. Rob checked his eyes and mouth and found swelling. 'What did he eat?' he asked.

The man's small wife answered, 'Nothing, he just had a coffee.'

'Does he have any allergies?'

'No, nothing.'

'Hello!' Rob shouted at the man, trying to get him to focus on him. 'Your body has gone into shock, mate. You're allergic to something. The ambulance is coming now. I need you to try to focus on me, look at me.' The man's tongue began to enlarge, and Rob could hear him gasping for air, so he hoisted him up and tried to unlock his jaw.

During this time, the mask watched Rob closely. It watched him hold the sick man's hand and mutter things to him, watched him shout over to Jasmine to ring the paramedics again and tell them to bring adrenalin. The mask watched him shout to get the wife and child out of here. It watched Rob say, 'You're going to be okay. Try and relax, mate, it's going to be okay.'

Rob realized the last time he had said these words was to his own son when he was trapped under a fallen roof. They had been on a weeklong holiday in Bali with his wife and her family. He and his son had gone into town for the day in search of some motorbikes to rent so they could ride around the island. After they found a man who was willing to rent to a 15-year-old, they grabbed a quick lunch in a small market. That's when the earthquake had hit.

At first, Rob thought the cheap table had a fault, but then it got stronger, and people started to shout and run. He tried to grab his son by the arm, but he had lost his grip. He shouted at him to follow. His son answered, so Rob ran out into the open road. Fallen buildings and live electrical poles surrounded him. Under his feet, the ground was cracked. He turned, anxious to find his son, but he couldn't see him. Immediately, he ran back into a haze of dust and debris. The thin tin roofs had fallen, and he could hear people shout and cry around him. He kept calling out his son's name until he heard him cry out. He rushed over and found him trapped under one of the roofs. He went to lift it off, but his son screamed, and he had to lower it again. He looked down at the metal plate and noticed that a large bolt had become lodged in his son's stomach. He tried to see how deep it went, but he couldn't. He then sat beside him, brushed away his hair, kissed his forehead, he tried to keep him stable. He took out his mobile and tried to call his wife, but reception was down. He started to shout loudly as his son started to drift in and out of consciousness. He heard ambulances and fire trucks and ran out to get their attention.

By the time he returned with help, his son was dead. The embassy made arrangements for him. His wife and her family were pronounced dead after the hotel collapsed, and the sea exploded. It was a massive earthquake, one that destroyed the region and would forever lie at the top of the list.

THE COFFEE SHOP MASQUERADE

At the coffee shop, Rob heard the ambulance before he saw it. It was trapped behind a lorry on Elgin Street, so the paramedics left and ran down the hill to the shop.

Rob greeted them and spoke fast. 'He has gone into shock. It's an allergy. You need to…'

The paramedics stared at him, 'You know this man?'

'No, I don't, but I'm a doctor. I know what this is.'

The paramedic opened one of their cases and took out a pen. Rob ripped at the man's trousers seam to clear a space for the pen, which one of the paramedics jabbed into him. The man let out a squeal, then relaxed. Rob stayed with him, he held his hand as they checked his eyes and mouth. They then lifted him up onto a stretcher and carried him down the steps to the ambulance, which was now blocking the entrance to the escalator. A large crowd had formed. Some people were making videos and taking pictures with their phones. Rob held his hand until they put him in.

'Let the wife and child in,' Rob said.

'You're not coming?' the paramedic asked.

'No, I used to be a doctor. I no longer practice.'

Ruth spoke to the paramedics and helped the wife and child into the ambulance. The wife then started to cry, and the small child sat dazed. The paramedics shouted at Ruth to get out of the way, which she did. The street was filled with people talking, pointing, and whispering. Some videoed images of Ruth — images that would be posted online later. The police arrived and tried unsuccessfully to assert some crowd control. Ruth, stunned by the crowd, walked back into the coffee shop, where she found Jasmine sobbing on the red couch and Rob bent over on a small table. A policeman was waiting for her.

'What happened?' he asked Ruth.

'I don't know. He ordered a large latte and a blueberry muffin and sat down. I then heard his wife scream and saw him collapse onto the floor in some sort of fit.'

'What did you do then?'

'I tried to help roll him over to his side, but that didn't seem to help so I…' Ruth stopped speaking and was suddenly felt tired, a reaction she often had to stress. She yawned loudly in front of the policeman.

He shouted at her, 'Hey, is this boring to you? A man nearly died in your shop, and you're yawning!'

Ruth jumped. She stared down at his military-like shoes. She wanted to lie down.

'So, what happened?'

Ruth explained – the wife, the coffee, the muffin, the child, she had rolled him, she didn't know why – it just seemed like a good idea. As she answered, she could see the mask above Jasmine's sobbing head. It seemed sad and woeful, and she thought back to the strange man who left it. He was in such a hurry and wanted to get rid of it. Maybe it's cursed, she thought. She felt sick.

'Are you the manager?'

'No, the manager has the day off.'

'We need to call him and your head office.'

Ruth wanted to ask, *why? Is it that serious? The man will be okay now. It's not like we killed him. I bet you wouldn't do this if he wasn't a tourist.* However, she stopped herself, already sensing the policeman's hostility toward her piercings and hair colors.

He walked away from her, and she noticed another policeman now guarding the door – no one was allowed to enter or exit.

She looked over at Rob, whose head was down. This large man now appeared so sad and vulnerable. She walked over and stood in front of him, waiting for him to acknowledge her, to look up into her eyes and smile, crack some crazy joke like he normally did, but he didn't. He sat frozen in some sort of shock.

She touched him out of her own need to connect.

'Thank you.' she whispered.

Rob looked up as if he'd awakened from a dream. Tears streamed down his face.

Ruth looked away, embarrassed for him. She never had seen a man cry before. Suddenly, she felt ashamed, believing she had provoked his tears.

He wiped his tears away and stared outside. The road now was closed and had become silent. He wondered about the old man for whom he had fetched tea — did he also go home? A voice sounded within him, *No one saves us but ourselves. No one can and no one may. We ourselves must walk the path.*

Ruth took the seat beside him and sat with him, unable to speak. They both listened to the policeman talking quickly on the phone, as if he was trying to beat his breath. Jasmine, uncomforted, still sobbed. In between breaths and sobs, short snippets of silence filled the shop. The bathroom door swung open, it emitted new life into the shop, a playful breeze trying to eradicate the situation's severity.

'Does it do that often?' Rob asked quietly, his red face still covered in tears, but his eyes present.

Ruth nodded. 'Ever since the mask arrived. Sometimes I think this place is haunted. We find cups all over the place.'

Rob looked up and saw the mask. He remembered his wife had wanted to buy something similar, a weird-looking empty face. 'It would look good in the pool house.' He heard her voice in his head and bent forward, clasping his large hands together. A voice sounded again within him, *Life is suffering, set your heart on doing good Mister Rob. Much kindness is needed here.*

Ruth leaned back. Rob's tears started to flow again, and she watched him try to pinch them away, he cursed their flow. He stood up tall and held his head up in an attempt to push them back into their ducts. Ruth heard him swear, then laugh — at his tears, at this emotion that seemed to control him.

He turned to her and smiled foolishly. 'I can't make it stop.' he confessed.

Ruth asked, 'Why are you crying?'

That made him cry more, and Ruth felt worse. Another policeman entered and whispered to the one on the phone. They looked over at the three of them suspiciously. Ruth was suddenly convinced they were all going to be arrested.

With Jasmine and Rob both crying, the policemen became confused, and after the one on the phone finished talking, he walked over to Ruth. 'Why are they crying?'

Ruth, afraid, shrugged her shoulders and shook her head.

The policeman went over to Rob. 'Are you okay?'

Rob didn't answer him but tried to nod through his tears.

'We want to say, 'thank you,' sir. You saved that man's life. You were right — he was allergic to something.'

Ruth stood up and went over to them both. She stood by anxiously, desperate to find out what it was. 'Well, what was it? What's he allergic to?'

'Spiders.'

'Spiders?'

'Yes, spiders. He went to Peng Chau yesterday, and apparently a spider jumped on his trousers, then when he was in here today, the spider bit him.'

'Bit him?'

'Yes.'

'The spider lived on him for that long?'

'Well, the doctors think that the spider became trapped in the crease of his trousers on the bottom and came out.'

'That's crazy.'

'Yes.'

THE COFFEE SHOP MASQUERADE

'But he'll be okay?' Rob asked.

The policeman awkwardly put his hand on Rob's upper arm. 'Don't worry. Thank you.'

He then turned to Ruth, 'I have spoken to your head office and explained. I tried to ring your manager, but I couldn't get through. But everything is okay now, so we're going to go, and you can reopen.'

Ruth walked the policemen out without saying anything. She closed the glass door behind them and locked it.

Jasmine, her eyes puffy and swollen, looked at her. 'What are you doing? We should reopen.'

'No, we shouldn't, we can't. Let's wait until Patrick arrives.'

'But look at all these customers' bags.'

Ruth looked at the shopping bags dotting the floor. 'They can come back another time.'

Rob sat down again. Jasmine left the red couch, returned to the counter, and turned off the machines. Ruth collected the half-drunken cups of coffee and untouched muffins. The bathroom door swung open again, and the cool breeze tickled her neck. She felt shaken, but almost excited. Rob let out a large sigh. She looked over at him and saw the tears had stopped.

She felt it was safe to venture over to him, she smiled and offered him an uneaten muffin. 'You want it?'

'No thanks,' he said, then smiled. She wanted to hug him but didn't. 'But I could do with a sweet coffee.'

'Sure.' She asked Jasmine to make one.

Rob watched the girls clean up silently. They have great precision and dedication, he thought. Not many people would stay and clean up after a day like today.

He stood up to help them. He emptied the bin and picked up sugar sachets. The floor, covered in loose sugar crystals, crunched beneath him. 'Have you a mop?'

'No, don't worry, the cleaning woman comes soon.'

Rob nodded and looked out to see whether he could determine what time it was the sky was still light. 'What time is it?'

'It's nearly 6.30.'

He passed the bin to Jasmine, who nodded. 'You girls going home now?'

'No, we have to wait for Patrick,' Ruth said.

'I can do that.'

'No thanks. I don't think he'd be happy if we weren't here.'

'Yeah, he does get a bit upset sometimes.'

Ruth and Jasmine giggled.

'We think it's the mother,' Ruth said.

'Oh, yeah, why? Is she always here?' Rob asked, remembering that she pointed at his stomach the first time she saw him.

'Don't know, but she drives him crazy.'

Ruth and Jasmine started to laugh, relieving the tension. Rob smiled with them and enjoyed their giggles. It was the first time they ever smiled at him or had any real conversation with him, despite his advances.

'You know you two are wasted in here.' he said cautiously.

'We are?' Jasmine replied.

'Yeah, you should be out there helping people with your smiles, instead of being in here serving coffee.'

'It's an okay job.'

'Yeah it is, but I have a better idea for you. I mean, you can try it once and see what you think, but I'd like it if you would.'

'What is it?' Ruth inquired.

'Well, it's helping people, making coffee, and talking to different people.'

'Uh huh, sounds strange.' Ruth answered staring at Jasmine.

'It's not. It's like a sanctuary.'

'What's that?' Jasmine asked.

'Like a place for people who have lost their way.' He watched their faces crinkle up. 'It's a place where people can be quiet.'

'Quiet?'

'Yes, quiet.'

'Why can't people be quiet at home?'

'Some people are afraid to be quiet, but we all need it. I just bought a place, you know, to help them be quiet. It's fantastic, just on the water next to Admiral.'

'But people can go to the temple for that.' Jasmine said.

'With religion, something is always expected of you. This is just for people to sit together, meditate, then have the option to read a poem or a piece of writing that has affected them, you know, meant something to them. Then they go home.'

'Sounds weird.'

'It isn't — it's to help people, allow them to take the time to focus on something else, something more important. There's no place like it here, and there needs to be.' He felt he was about to reiterate the speech that he had given to the bank managers this morning, but stopped, he lifted up his palms, raised his shoulders, and said, 'I just want to help people.'

There was silence. He almost expected them to laugh or smirk at him like the bankers had today, but they didn't — they only looked at each other, then back at him.

'Is it just for foreigners?' Ruth asked.

'Nope, also locals and mainlanders, which is why I could use you two.'

'Oh, I don't know. I think I'd be afraid of crazy people,' Ruth said.

'They aren't that crazy — they're like me. You think I'm crazy?'

Jasmine and Ruth looked at each other and burst out laughing.

'Okay maybe that wasn't the best example.' Rob hung his head.

Although Ruth was unable to truly understand his project's concept, she felt drawn to his idea, sensing his passion. Anything would be better than this, she thought.

'Good money?' she said.

He lifted his head and spoke seriously, 'Better than here, I guarantee it, and good opportunities for education, and it's in the best location, right by the water. Good energy.'

Ruth looked at Jasmine, and they nodded at each other.

Ruth replied, 'Okay, maybe we'll come over and see? Only to see for now.'

'Great,' Rob said, he took out his name card again.

'No need. We already have it, remember?' Jasmine said.

'Yes, of course.'

Suddenly, there was heavy banging on the door. The three of them jumped at seeing Patrick trying to open the door. Ruth walked over and unlocked the door, and Patrick entered, shouting at her. Rob smiled at Patrick, who ignored him. Patrick lifted his arms in annoyance, he threw questions at them and was quick to highlight their defects.

Rob winked at Jasmine and Ruth and walked out into the bright evening. Staunton Street was once again alive, but he didn't walk down there, he decided to walk past the gym.

There, he bumped into Kimberley with her oversized bag. Her face shone as if she had scrubbed it clean.

'Sorry, didn't see you there,' he said.

'No problem.' she replied. She recognized him but was unable to place him.

'Have a nice evening,' Rob said.

'Yeah, you too.'

Rob bounced down the hill and climbed over the dented rails on Hollywood Road. He stopped by a small alley bar he liked and ordered a beer, then before long, someone shouted at him.

THE COFFEE SHOP MASQUERADE

'Hey, you, with the big time grand plan.'

Rob started to giggle and got up. He held out his hand, and Monkey shook it.

'Long time no see, Monkey!'

'Yeah, I've been around, looking for this strange mask I lost a few years ago — thought I saw it recently.'

Rob stared at him. 'You know, I just saw a weird mask in that coffee shop up the hill.'

'Really? What kind of mask?'

'Funny looking thing, sort of Italian looking. The girls in the shop said the mask is haunted and causes the bathroom doors to open.'

Monkey stared at him dumbfounded. 'Well, that sounds like my mask!'

'Go and see it — it's on the shelf.'

And with that, Monkey got up and started to run away.

Rob called after him. 'Hey, Monkey, Monkey! The coffee shop is closed.'

But Monkey ignored him. *It won't get away from me now. I've fought worse things than a silly mask.*

The coffee shop was closed, but Monkey peered through the window, he saw it!

Hmm, I'm coming for you! He looked around. Too many people, he thought, I'll get in trouble again, then I'll be stuck in that stupid peach orchard for another five centuries. He stared at the mask. I'll find a way to get you, just you wait.

11

The Coffee Shop Masquerade

The wise are not learned.
The learned are not wise.
–Tao Te Ching

Kimberley had always known that she didn't want to stay in Canada. When she was younger, she sat at home most weekends and watched movies and documentaries about places far away. Her grandmother would sit beside her and tell her, 'Don't waste your time here like I did. Get out and live a little.' So, she did.

When she entered the coffee shop today, it was busy, and she didn't know where to sit. She had left work half an hour early to enjoy some time reading through the *New Yorker* she had received yesterday in the post and decided that the coffee shop on the corner would be the best choice to spend the late afternoon, as it was normally empty when she looked in from the escalator on her way home from work. However, it was oddly busy today.

The crowd waiting for their beverages surrounded the counter, they stared slightly menacingly at the stressed staff and blocked Kimberley's view.

She quickly sensed that something was wrong, as exhausted people dressed in crinkled suits and skirts moaned in annoyance. Absorbing their mood, she thought of other places she could go to instead but decided against them. It seemed pointless to go to the coffee shop in Central—all the way back down there—when she was already halfway home. Thus, she reluctantly joined the back of what she thought was a line.

The machines around her sounded noisily, and a light above them flickered sporadically, desperate to find a more suitable mood for the afternoon. Then the music sounded very loudly and she, along with the rest of the crowd, jumped. It quickly readjusted to a lower volume, then Kimberley realized what had happened—a short-lived power outage.

Walking through Soho, she had noticed that the escalator had stopped, and the road was dark when normally it was already lit with its muted rainbow of signs. She smiled down at the wooden floor, remembering the many power outages she had endured as a child, dark evenings with candles and her grandmother and Haga, their cat that couldn't purr. She liked the feeling when the power was off; it made her feel secure—things were out of her control, and all she had to do was be.

The music started to become more upbeat, and she felt her shoulders start to sway as the crowd began to vanish. Out of habit she looked down at her watch. Time was ticking by, and soon she'd be forced to think about dinner. Questioning her need for coffee this late in the day, she quickly told herself, no, I want a coffee. I deserve a coffee, and after all, it could be a celebratory coffee. This forced her to bite down on her lip anxiously. Her face acted in constant alliance with her thoughts, giving away her current state and making her appear sometimes unintentionally comical. She looked up at the ceiling and the dark wooden fan that wasn't moving, she noticed a small spider sat at the end of its gold beaded wire surveying all those below.

She sighed. It was finally decided today that she was getting a 10 percent raise, but this came with more responsibility. She was afraid of any more work, but desperately needed the money, which would allow her to travel more. She'd found that being confined to the city every weekend doing laundry and watching pointless T.V shows had rapidly depleted her ambition to see the world. Her recent trip home to Canada to see her grandmother had reminded her that there was a world outside of this city, with its snow-filled trees and strong fresh winds that provided a different stimulating existence. She had found herself able to think clearly again.

Solitude is what she thought she really needed—the one thing that could cure her mind—and since she had returned, she searched online for meditation retreats to find a place where no noise was a rule, and she could just be quiet. It was hard to be silent here, as she often felt people stared, and judged her.

Moving here had been a good idea at the time—to be with him, her ex—but after he had left her for some local girl who apparently understood him more, there didn't seem much point. He had left her a year ago, and since then, she hadn't met anyone. Her job kept her busy, but the rent now was destroying her chances of having a real life outside of coffees and cinema tickets. She shuddered thinking about him. He took this local girl back to Canada and paraded her around town like a prize pig, her grandmother told her over the phone—not much of her to parade, a skinny sort of girl with crooked eyes. These unkind words from her grandmother helped to ease the blow of their sudden marriage. It devastated her to think that he had recovered from them so quickly.

There were many guys whom she was attracted to, but most were unreachable strangers, and although she would do her best to flirt and give her hair that flip, it rarely worked, and they never returned her advances. She didn't like to be on her own, but somehow, in this city, it felt like everyone was alone even if they weren't. It was safe to be alone here, as there weren't many special occasions that one had to attend, where you feel like an outcast for being single. Many residents were single, and even at the seemingly friendly meetings, there was always an underlying brutality that people wanted to remain alone, bask in their own independence, their situation — their feelings safely masked by their positions.

But this all changed recently for Kimberley after she had hooked up with someone when she was back home — someone younger, but eager. As if on cue, her phone rang. She looked down at the foreign number and blushed. It was him, and he was up late. She walked outside the coffee shop and stood beside a row of taxis. She heard his voice.

'Hello, beautiful.' he said.

She grinned into the air. 'Hello, yourself.'

'I miss you.'

She nodded, forgetting to reply.

'Kimberley, are you still there?'

'Yes, sorry, just surprised. What are you doing up?'

'I couldn't sleep after last night — can't stop thinking about you.'

'Well, that's nice.'

'Could you sleep?'

'Yes, but it took a while.'

'I miss you when I'm awake and when I'm asleep. How fucked up is that?'

'I know.'

'Ugh, anyway just wanted to wish you a good evening.'

'Thank you Michael, and you also have a good day.'

'Thanks, I will — love you, Kim.'

'You too — bye, Michael.'

She pressed down the red button and felt herself blush, but

quickly shooed it away silently, she thought don't be stupid, no one knows anything. It's only a bit of fun, she had told herself, but now, after that phone call, she felt off-balance once more. She walked back into the sanctuary of the coffee shop that blocked out the roar of the city. The line was still long, and she rejoined the back of it.

Why did he call? Everything was okay before he called. I never thought it would turn out like this. Kimberley had met Michael on a dating app that she had downloaded on a whim when she returned home during the holidays. She was only in Toronto for two nights before she headed north toward home and decided to try the app out. She had made a match within the first 10 minutes and agreed to meet Michael downtown for a drink. He was fresh out of college, unemployed, but came from a wealthy family and was seven years younger than her. She wasn't looking for anything in particular, but immediately liked him when he offered her his jumper when she complained how cold it was. They discovered quickly that they were from very similar towns and talked for a while about life, desires, and distance. He came back to her room, they kissed, and he stayed with her the two nights she was there. It felt enjoyable, not seedy—just what she needed. It didn't evoke the danger of love, not from her side, but she could see that he wanted more, and she had been unsuccessfully been trying to distance herself from him since she got back to Hong Kong, but it was hard because once again, she was alone.

Every day since then, she tried to convince herself to call it off, but secretly enjoyed that he wanted her so badly. Only last week, she dubiously succumbed to his requests for naked photos, and they had just started to have online sex. She kept him a secret. It made her smile to think that some boy from home thought about her in that way, but it wouldn't last—it couldn't.

She smiled, remembering the look on his face after they stopped kissing. However, these tender thoughts stopped abruptly when she felt someone standing beside her.

'Here you go.'

She jumped when she realized that it was Patrick. She looked at the people in front of her, but they were too busy staring at the fresh pastries that had arrived.

'What is it?' she asked, after being handed a red ceramic mug filled with blackness.

'Your normal. Black Ethiopian blend, one sugar.' He grinned proudly at her, his arm stretched out clutching the coffee.

'Oh, thanks,' she muttered, confused, 'but I,' then she looked down at the pockets that surrounded her bag, 'but should I pay you now or wait till I get to the counter?'

Patrick smiled back and closed his eyes, 'No, no need. This is free for you.'

'Free?' She smiled.

'Yes, free.'

'Oh thanks, that's very nice, thank you.' She took it from him, and he almost bowed at the mere honor of serving her coffee.

'You're welcome.'

She was about to walk away when he said, 'You had a good day?'

'Yes, thanks, and you?' she asked.

'Yes,' he nodded, 'very, very good—very, very busy,' he repeated.

'Well, that's good.' She wanted to leave and try and make it to the red couch, which suddenly was empty, but she stood still and felt as if she should say something else. 'Are you sure I can't pay you for this?'

'No, please, I can give away coffee. I'm the manager.'

'The manager—I had no idea, wow.' She didn't know what

else to say. She knew he was the manager, as he always was shouting and ordering the girls around and looking around to see whether the tables were clean.

'Yes,' he said confidently, 'it's responsibility, but I like it.'

She nodded politely and turned away from him before he could ask her anything else. She mouthed 'thanks' and headed to the red couch. She sat down and took out her magazine, desperate to hide her embarrassment from receiving all this attention. Does this mean I can't come here anymore? Is he going to become a pest?

After she took the first sip, Kimberley suddenly felt tired, as if she had eaten too much sugar fast. Her head grew cloudy, and she felt that if she could just lie down on the red couch, she'd sleep deeply and be hard to awaken. Too many late nights conversing through the screen had left her isolated from the world, and when faced with real humans, outside of the shy strangers at work, she felt exhausted and confused by the rhythm of life.

Last weekend, she stayed in—typing, dreaming, waiting for Michael to call. He seemed to be able to encourage her to think of herself once more, life was not just about her job and the need to succeed. But if she was being realistic about this relationship, she knew it wasn't going to go anywhere and had to stop, but she did love the attention. Sometimes she felt as if she was pretending to be someone else. She stared straight ahead at the mask on the shelf—*what happens to the old masks when we start to wear new ones?*

Patrick's eyes followed her. He had wanted to keep talking to her, ask her something else, or tell her about all the responsibilities he had. He could tell her about that weird dream he had last night, in which he was stuck in a great forest, and he had come across a tiger that told him to watch out for Monkey. Dreams are so crazy.

He wanted to keep their conversation going, but then his mother walked in, and his mood instantly was dampened.

Kimberley couldn't understand what was being said between Patrick and the old woman, but she looked upon his miserable face with pity as the old woman squawked at him through their common language. He tried to motion for her to leave, but the old woman wouldn't and remained defiant. She proceeded to wander around the coffee shop, examining the neat shelves of Thermos coffee cups. She bent over and rudely stared into the tourists' faces as their orders lined the counter. She played with the small drawer filled with ribbed warmth protectors, she shouted to Jasmine behind the counter, but Jasmine ignored her.

Patrick trailed behind her, incessantly asking her to leave, but she firmly shook her head and walked over to the fern that sat in the corner. She pinched it, then shouted something over to the staff. Jasmine and Coco broke out into laughter, and Patrick frowned. She stopped and pointed at the mask. She spoke very low and serious, and Patrick shook his head. She looked at the mask confused, then the bathroom door opened by itself.

Kimberley watched this out of the corner of her eye, the magazine helping to protect her stare. By the looks of it, this woman was someone's relative or some local crazy woman whom they tolerate. Kimberley grew alarmed when the old woman headed toward the red couch and sat down beside her. This seemed to be the last straw as Patrick rushed over and tried to persuade her to move. The old woman looked at Kimberley and started to argue with him.

It was like watching a badly dubbed silent movie. Kimberly could understand the body language, but not one word of what was being said. She looked down, embarrassed for Patrick as the woman didn't move, but sat rebellious, clutching her cheap tan bag. Kimberley decided that she would leave instead, as it felt like she was in the middle of some family dispute, so she put her magazine away and started to pack up.

Patrick watched her and said, 'Please, don't worry, so sorry, so sorry.'

The old woman laughed at his apologies.

Kimberley turned and flicked her fringe. 'Don't worry, it's fine. I need to go home anyway.'

'Thank you,' he said. 'You very kind.'

'Thank you for the coffee.' she replied, then turned her back on him, she criticized herself for even coming in there — this would be the last time.

Patrick stood staring wistfully at her, then jumped as he heard his mother squawk again, this time it was about Chris, who had just entered the coffee shop. He was wearing shorts when it was only 50 degrees Fahrenheit outside. Patrick hushed her and returned to the counter.

The old woman moved from the red couch and walked toward Chris. She barked something at him, that forced him to jump. He didn't know whether she was directing a comment at him or someone else, but she moved out of his view quickly, so he assumed that it didn't concern him.

———∽∽———

The shop felt different today, Chris thought as he looked around, like a scene of a physical fight. It felt tense and alive. He stood in line looking around, trying to figure out the change that had taken place. He looked up and saw the mask on the shelf, it appeared to be on the edge, ready to drop off at any second.

———∽∽———

THE COFFEE SHOP MASQUERADE

Kimberley, walked down the stairs and felt a slight touch on her shoulder. She turned around and saw a breathless Grace smiling at her.

'Hi there.' Grace said. She had entered the shop in an attempt to stop the damaging thoughts that flowed throughout her, that sickened her stomach. She saw the back of Kimberley's head, and was drawn to her. It had been a while since they had seen each other, but she really wanted to see a friend, someone else outside of the life she had now chosen to live. Fueled with anxiety, she wanted to cry when Kimberley went to hug her.

'Hello, you,' she said tenderly.

They embraced, and Kimberley felt drips of emotion fall off Grace onto her like small specks of snow. As they looked into each other's eyes, she sensed that Grace was in the middle of some transformation — she was alive, but vulnerable, and Kimberley felt tingles begin to dimple on her own skin. She wanted to ask her whether someone died.

'Let's sit down,' Grace whispered, unable to speak any louder.

'Umm, I don't know if we should.' She tried to point out the old woman who had just disappeared into the haunted bathroom.

'Please, Kimberley,' Grace almost whimpered.

'What is it?'

'I'm in trouble.'

Kimberley looked down at her stomach — was she pregnant? She didn't know what to say to her but knew from her former coworker that it wasn't good. Grace rarely opened up emotionally, everything was always so perfect with her, so Kimberley sat back on the red couch, alert, her legs facing the small table. Grace was about to start when another acquaintance of hers walked in.

'Oh my god,' she said softly, then louder, 'Emma, over here.' Kimberley sat and watched her alter her stance. Grace sat up and swallowed whatever she was about to say, then she stood up, regal and embraced Emma like an honored guest. Kimberley thought *I guess we change masks whenever it's necessary, for our own protection.*

Emma smiled. 'Hi, Grace. Wow! It's been a while.'

'Yes, it has! Sorry I haven't called — been so busy.'

'Yeah, me too.'

'So, how's everything?'

'Great! You know, the same.' Grace looked helplessly into Kimberley's eyes. 'You remember Kimberley, don't you?'

'Yes, of course, from your birthday!' And she kissed her cheek, 'Hi, Kim, how are you?'

'Good, thanks, and you?'

'The same,' she replied, relaying Grace's words. These small words protected each of them, they plugged up the thick surge of awkward feelings that would come out later evoking feelings of stumbling around blind in dark alleys.

'Great!' Emma said. Afraid to go any further into a conversation, she added, 'Well, I better go and order. I'm meeting Sophia in an hour.'

'Sophia? Are you still friends with her?' Grace said, not thinking.

'Yes.' Emma looked down, embarrassed. She remembered that night she and Grace had gone out for dinner when she had confided in Grace about her real feelings about Sophia; her ex, Alex; and being away from home. Grace also had returned those thoughts, but over time, they each had abandoned these truths and condemned them to the back of shelves, not to be seen nor touched.

'Yes, I am. Well, you know.'

Grace nodded, realizing that she was no longer capable of judging anyone if they were unhappy. She had started to marvel at what people did to feel better and worthy to survive.

THE COFFEE SHOP MASQUERADE

Grace looked around the coffee shop while Emma elaborated on Sophia's niceties. Her eyes locked with Chris' who sat at the table in the corner by the door, his attention was firmly on Emma. Grace caught his eyes, and he sheepishly smiled at them, realizing he had just been caught. Grace copied his grin and looked at Emma, wondering if she knew. Perhaps there was a new secret man in her life and that she had just interrupted their secret rendezvous.

She nodded along to Emma's words, then quietly grabbed her arm and whispered excitedly, 'There's a guy over there who's looking at you.'

'What?'

'A guy over there in the corner.'

Emma nodded as if she knew, but she suddenly stopped talking and turned slowly. Chris beamed at her, and she gave a small smile back.

The three women now joined in this event, all started to giggle, releasing their individual tensions.

'So, Emma, got a new man in your life?' Grace asked.

'No, I don't think so,' Emma laughed, obviously thrilled to be at the center of things for once.

As they stood there whispering and laughing, Patrick's mom circulated around the coffee shop anew, complaining about the dust and poor décor. She sized up the mask, there's something wrong with it—it doesn't belong here. Bad luck, she had told her son. *Something that doesn't belong will always cause problems.* She picked up a lone cup that sat underneath a table. Why is this here? She looked toward the women standing beside the red couch, watching them laugh with each other and she became jealous and sad. She once had friends like that when she was young, they laughed spontaneously over the smallest things. She looked over toward her hard-working son, who appeared so removed from laughter and joy, and she remembered tenderly how wonderful it felt to really laugh.

Chris continued to smile over at them and waited for Emma to leave the safety of the other two women. At least he managed to get a smile out of her. He was happy with his decision to come back to this coffee shop, he had hoped he might see her again. It must be destiny, he thought, then he shuddered at the word—it wasn't one he normally used. It must have been after watching that sappy romantic comedy last night with that hot chick looking for her destiny—he must have absorbed it then. Anyway, destiny—he thought, what the hell, maybe it is, it's definitely better than sincere

Patrick banged away at the coffee machine, trying to meet Kimberley's eyes, but only saw that they were filled with laughter, and he turned away, happy that she was happy.

Andrew walked in and went straight for the line. He didn't want to be in here long, as he wanted to go to the gym for an hour and return to a home that was now thankfully free of family visitors. He thought about his aunt and uncle—Charlotte and William- in their five-star hotel in Singapore, sucking down Singapore Slings and avoiding real conversation, and he felt bad that he hadn't made more of an effort with them when they were here.

He became distracted when he saw Jasmine explaining something to a timid girl swamped in an oversized apron. She held a large collection of dirty plates and coffee cups, some of their remains streamed down her hands in the form of coffee droplets that fell silently on the floor, which she ignored as she nodded frantically to Jasmine's calm instructions. Must be new staff, he assumed, and they do need some. However, he grew annoyed that the line didn't seem to be moving. He only wanted a bottle of water. He found that the water in the fountain at the gym tasted too much like metal and preferred to drink out of plastic bottles. He exhaled with irritation as the large woman in front of him kept changing her order. First, it was three iced lattes with whipped cream to go, then three normal lattes to stay here, then a cookie — no, a biscotti instead, three of them.

Chris, spotted Andrew, his new acquaintance he met at football and went up directly behind him and touched his shoulder. They greeted each other, both gently bounced on their toes, and Andrew forgot about his irritation.

Grace's phone rang, and she dived into her pocket to retrieve it, then Kimberley quietly noticed that she appeared disappointed with the caller and didn't answer it.

Emma couldn't look over at Chris watching them. She was afraid that someone was playing a trick on her — probably one of Sophia's hot men, she suspected — not recognizing his face from Sunday.

Chris, now finished with the small talk from Andrew about the football game on Sunday, looked in Emma's direction again, but her face had withdrawn in the refuge of the women. He was about to return to his seat when he watched Andrew head over toward them. He appeared confident as he kissed one of them on the cheek. Chris stood up—shocked but elated. He didn't know what he should do, but decided that this was his chance, so he walked over and introduced himself.

'Hi, I'm Chris.'

'Oh yes, you haven't met Chris. He's new on our football team—this is James' wife, Grace,' Andrew said.

'Oh right. Hi, I'm Grace.'

Chris nodded at her, smiling.

Grace, picked up on his interest in Emma, promptly introduced the rest of the women. The two men smiled and nodded hellos. Andrew was afraid as he recognized Emma as being with that weird Australian girl who had accosted him on the stairs outside the gym, but he quickly relaxed as he saw her grow as uncomfortable as he was.

Finished with introductions, silence suddenly loomed around them like a foul smell, each desperate to break its stench.

'Have you been here long?' Grace asked Chris.

'Umm, well nearly a year.'

The question enabled them to start to converse once again. They then went on to exchange brief synopses of their present lives—why they were there, where they used to live, how long they were staying—each question quickly followed the last, with tiny answers that mushroomed into bigger thoughts. Did you like it? Mostly nods, small and shy smiles to each other, each told their story and voiced their opinions and narratives. They enjoyed this talk, it being a common method of survival. It felt as if they were young again before the city had showered them with privilege, making them believe that they were something better than they were, with their hired help and low taxes.

The machines sounded around them, they emitted loud noises as they frothed, percolated, and stirred. Strangers came and went that late afternoon, then there was a quiet calm. However, they remained oblivious to it all, they remained on the worn red couch, the thin coffee table littered with their beverages.

Andrew decided against going to the gym, after he found normal nontaxing conversation to be a better way to relax.

Grace bought some cookies that they all shared, a childish treat to encourage friendship.

Emma sent a message to Sophia, she lied and said she was stuck at work and would be late.

Debussy played in the background, soft, luxurious notes bounced off the walls, filling the shop with a strong breeze. The mask watched them all with interest. Their voices grew in volume during the lull between musical tracks. Insignificant words and thoughts masked emptiness and homesickness, and little was discussed over the truly ailing thoughts about lost lives and odd occurrences. The pressing feelings of ambition, of needing to acquire more in every aspect of their lives, remained safely alive behind their noisy laughs, like the furniture that surrounded them. They appeared practical, necessary, but non-offensive.

Their voices relaxed the mask, overly anxious that today its owner would return. It finally sat back and viewed them curiously on the red couch. Such a big gathering. Same thoughts and same old fears and reservations as those who lived before. The mask considered whether it should compel them to do odd, strange things, cause havoc. Shaken up their mood, like it did with Charlotte, but then it noticed their language altered. They started to say different words. They started to voice how they were feeling inside, some were afraid, some were lonely, this city was hard. They voiced these feelings without fear of judgment. The mask hadn't seen man speak so openly to newly acquired acquaintances in a long time. The mask eavesdropped, distracted by their realities.

Chris finally spoke to Emma while the other three let them talk freely. She studied his face, not out of attraction or curiosity, but from the unusual thought that she had dreamed about him, that he had appeared to her in a dream some nights before, his face and hands made the same movements as they were now, she stared politely at him while being quietly amazed at her mind. She then remembered him from last Sunday with the strange girl, but she didn't want to ask about her and grinned as he asked about her job, her apartment, and whether she went out a lot. He's nice, she thought, but not exactly my type.

He didn't notice her skin when he spoke to her; it was as if her spots disappeared as she told him about Stanley Market and the cheap bed linen she bought there.

Patrick's mother left, colliding with Rob on her way out.
Rob called out, 'Hey, lady, watch where you're going!'

Others in the shop ignored him and failed to see the smile that his entrance brought to Jasmine's face.

Patrick breathed a sigh of relief, and those on the red couch beckoned him over, asking him about her.

'Your mother?' Kimberley asked.

'Yes, my mother. I'm sorry.' His eyes looked shattered, making Kimberley think she would return; she knew what it was like to have an overly critical mother.

'Well, she seemed nice,' said Grace, awkwardly.

'No, she's not, but she's very proud, and so she come here and see what the coffee shop is like every day.'

'Every day?' said Kimberley, surprised, as this was the first time she had seen her.

'And what does she think?' asked Grace.

'She said she think it okay, but it not good because, umm, because of where it is.'

'You mean Soho?'

'No, not Soho — because it is not level.' Patrick tried to show a horizontal line using his hands.

'Not level?' Chris asked.

'No, of course, it's halfway up,' said Emma triumphantly.

'Or halfway down if you look at it another way,' Chris retorted.

'Is that the same, you think, as saying a glass is half full or half empty?' Andrew enquired.

'I'm not sure,' Chris said.

Then they all laughed and started to discuss the theory behind empty glasses. Patrick looked lost as they talked fast over each other.

Rob sat at the small table beneath them. He grabbed an old car magazine and started to flip through it. Hearing their loud conversation and deep laughter, he smiled. They didn't see

Jasmine walk over to him with a coffee and free muffin, and they didn't witness her tilt her head to the side and giggle when he asked if it was nonfat. Rob listened in on their conversation's familiar words and topics and yearned to tell them on the red couch that there's so much more that it's almost impossible to explain, but he felt they would just think him mad.

An hour passed, and the evening arrived outside. Crowds began to fill the street, ready to consume wine and cocktails at happy hour. Loud beats and overly sexualized lyrics sounded from the street's bars, enticing people to enter and enjoy their special atmosphere. Locals sipped on fruit juices while Western girls drank tequila shots.

The group on the red couch didn't turn to look out of the dark window, but sat comfortably, surrounded by caffeine. Time lost its impending importance. Minor friendships grew out of past stories and revelations in hopes of making safe alliances for the up-and-coming present, each tore off a layer as they relaxed in stimulant aroma and the safety of language. They felt secure here in a refuge for foreigners in a foreign place.

They didn't notice Patrick move away from them and return to the counter crushed—they only turned when the haunted bathroom door opened and shut suddenly, the mask now back to its mischief. They took that as a sign, as people looked at the time, and each rose to leave. The others in the coffee shop left, and Patrick told Jasmine it was okay if she left a bit early.

None of them turned to acknowledge Patrick, who wiped down the empty tables. The air was filled with light caressing goodbyes, exchanged numbers, and promises of meetings. Each departed ready to look down, some down at the stairs, others at a magazine or a phone, as the escalator transported them toward their apartments in the sky. Invigorated after exchanging stories, they each felt a space opening in them once more, allowing the

THE COFFEE SHOP MASQUERADE

insanity of thoughts to circulate their way throughout their minds again, creating events and pressing upon brain cells.

Although they had left, their words seemed to hang in the air above the red couch. Patrick, now alone, walked over to it feeling the remains of their invisible vibrations. He decided to sit down on the red couch and soak up their presence. He let their hidden movements absorb into his skin. How he would like to be a stranger in a land free from family and commitments. How lucky they are! He looked over at the counter and the mask. His mother had said it was bad luck, it didn't belong and that he needed to get rid of it because nothing good will come from it. He got up and went toward it after locking the front door. He picked the mask up and examined the small writing on its back, but he couldn't make sense of it. He went back toward the red couch with the mask and sighed, he then leaned back and placed the mask on his face.

It was snug, but it fit him well. He then started to feel tingles and small vibrations, and he sat up. *Show me outside*, a voice sounded. He held the mask to his face as he walked toward the front door.

He opened it and faced the city, which ignored him like an intoxicated man drunk on adrenalin. He looked down the road toward the crowds that sipped their promotional beverages on the tiny uneven sidewalks.

His hearing greatly improved, he heard everything, coughs, whispers, sighs and felt laughter as it moved toward him, like artificial warmth from a small heater. He heard a helicopter hover mile above him behind the blanket of clouds, taxi honks that sounded like angry ducks, and late people shout out to those waiting for them.

He looked up, trying to see past the escalator, but his view was distracted by two children that hung out of an low-rise apartment window, they attempted to dampen the heads that walked down with water guns. He tried to see further toward the peak, but the monumental constructions guarded it like a modern Great Wall.

Patrick stared out of the mask and thought about his customers coming together on the red couch, and how he wanted to be there with them, but the voice sounded again within him, *the strong and great sink down. The soft and weak rise up. Long-winded speech is exhausting, better to stay centered.*

The voice surprised him, but he liked it. He heard a noise above him.

'Hey, you, down there in the mask!'

Patrick gazed up and saw a man jump down from a window wearing a Monkey King costume.

Patrick took off the mask and stared straight at him. The costume was incredible, and he thought he must be in a movie, but then remembered his dream, about the tiger and Monkey. Patrick rushed back in the coffee shop and turned to quickly shut the coffee shop door on him, but Monkey was too strong.

'Don't be a fool!' Monkey grabbed him by his neck and carried him toward the counter like he was a cat. He then put him down.

'I'm Monkey, the great sage equaling heaven, and that's my mask. I'd like it back, please.'

Patrick was astounded. 'Great sage equaling heaven?' he mumbled

'Yes, that's me, and I'd like my mask back.'

Patrick stared at the mask. 'Are you sure?'

'Yes,' Monkey replied, grabbing it from him.

Monkey examined the mask. 'You're not getting away from me this time, so much trouble for such a worthless thing.' He turned to leave, but then came face-to-face with Mario, who appeared thin and visibly shaken.

'Please, my mask. I need the mask. Per favore!'

Monkey shook his head. 'It isn't your mask—it's mine.'

'No,' Mario replied, crying, 'no, I need it, I haven't been able to, well, I haven't been well, Monkey. This mask was the only thing giving me any sort of balance. I come all the way back from Italy. I need it—it cries out to me in my sleep.'

'This old thing?' Monkey held it up. 'Made by a witch, this was. I think she put a spell on it. I found it—well, I found…' And then Monkey heard a loud ringing in his ears. 'OUCH! OUCH!!! Okay, Okay, Okay. Stop it!' He looked at Patrick and Mario. 'Ugh, I can't lie. I stole the mask from the witch. It was supposed to be her death mask, but I liked the look of it, so I took it. Thought I could sell it for some beer.' Monkey glanced at them sheepishly. 'It was a long time ago—I was younger then, still trying to figure out what I was supposed to do. Us gods, we're no longer as important.'

Mario looked at Monkey and held out his hand shaking. 'Please, Monkey may I have it?'

Monkey stared at the mask. The mask glared back. *Let me go back*, a small voice said. 'Oh, well, if you want it so badly.' He handed it over to him.

'Grazie, Grazie mille, Monkey.'

Monkey grinned . 'I renounce my ownership of this mask. It's now yours, Mario, but remember:

Extreme love exacts a great price.

Many possessions entail a heavy loss.

Know what is enough.

Abuse nothing.

Know when to stop.

Harm nothing.

This is how to last a long time.'

Mario smiled back, though confused by the words. He nodded and started to back away from Monkey and Patrick while whispering to the mask, 'Time to go home.' He rushed out and walked fast toward Veronica, his sister who was waiting in a restaurant further down the street for him. He grabbed hold of the mask tightly, *Nonna she is coming home, she has had her adventure.* He thought now everything will be okay again. It had been hard for him; he had gotten sick and then the nightmares came. The mask gave him balance, it meant more to him then he realized, and he had been suffering in all areas of his life since he left it behind. *Now it is a fresh start Nonna.*

Monkey sighed and shook his head, man and his silliness over items. He grinned at Patrick, with his yellow animal teeth. 'Now, young man, you sell beer?'

About The Author

T.A. Morton is an Irish/Australian writer. Previously, she worked as a journalist and editor for Longman Pearson in Hong Kong. In 2020, she was shortlisted for the Virginia Prize for Fiction and the Bridport Prize. She has a masters in Crime and Thriller writing from the University of Cambridge. Her novel Someone is Coming was published by Monsoon Books in August 2022 and has been optioned for television.

www.ingramcontent.com/pod-product-compliance
Lightning Source LLC
LaVergne TN
LVHW030321070526
838199LV00069B/6521